THE

ABSENCE

OF

PREDATORS

IN

THE

ABSENCE

OF

PREDATORS

BY VINNIE WILHELM

**RESCUE
+PRESS**

Rescue Press, Milwaukee 53212
Copyright © 2011 by Vinnie Wilhelm
Printed in the United States of America

www.rescue-press.org

Cover design by Skye McNeill
Cover photograph by Karen Klugman
Book design by Rescue Press
First Edition

ISBN: 978-0-9844889-1-9

TABLE OF CONTENTS

WHITE DOG

On Monday night I dreamt that a silent white dog would run through the dusty streets of Samalayuca at dawn, circling twice around the fountain in the church square and then disappearing north up the Zaragoza road. It happened the next morning almost exactly as I had foreseen, except that in my dream the dog ran counterclockwise around the fountain, while in reality it was the opposite. We were saddling the horses outside the hacienda of Don Ernesto Fernandez. The dog's pale fur shone like ice in the morning sun. "It is a good sign," Don Ernesto decided, "an omen of luck for the journey to Tularosa." He stood fingering the links of his silver watch fob for a moment and then bid us a solemn farewell. I told no one of my premonition.

That night I dreamt of the shooting of a horse. The next day Miguel Ignacio's horse stumbled as we crossed a dry arroyo, breaking its leg. Miguel Ignacio wept as he pulled the trigger, and continued weeping as he climbed onto the back of my mount, wrapping his thick arms around me and grasping the bottoms of my crossed bandoleers. "That horse was more to me than any woman has ever been," he said, and we knew he meant it. He was not ashamed that we should see his bitter tears. That night I dreamt that whores would sing to us of love torn apart by violence.

The next day we rode into San Elizario in a rainstorm, a raw wind bringing news of winter from the north. We were cold. Wet clothes clung to our bodies. It was an evening to forget ourselves in drink. In the Agua Dulce saloon local men toasted us out of fear and we drank with our guns on, remembering our comrades who no longer kept the trail in this world. Madame Ibarra got on the tin piano and her girls came down the broad stairway in white nightgowns, raising their sweet young voices in song. They sang of Pancho Villa's woman, waiting in Ascencion with powdered thighs while her lover bled in the dust at Parral. In the song he dies thinking of her. I do not doubt that it was so. I made a beast of myself atop a girl who could have been no more than twelve. Her skin smelled of cactus milk; she did not have the deep earth aroma of tilled soil. Pancho Villa's woman would have smelled like the freshly plowed fields. I fell asleep and dreamt that my wife would give birth to a child with two heads.

Of course I have no wife. All day this problem vexed me as we rode north under a frigid sun, and I wondered if perhaps the rigors of a brutal life had at last made off with my reason. Snow in the mountains, drifting over the bones of dead cattle—we would press on through the night to reach Tularosa by sunrise. We would strike with the advantage of surprise. In the evening an icy brook crossed the trail and we stopped there to fill our canteens. Crouching beside José Gallardo on the bank, watching the water rush across his callused hands, I was startled to recognize them as the very hands I had used to deliver the child in my dream—such powerful hands, and yet so gentle as they eased the two small heads into our desolate world. The stream caressed his iron knuckles; high above a vulture sang, and I understood of a sudden that the wife of whom I had dreamt was in fact José Gallardo's. I realized that José Gallardo's dream must have wandered away from him in the night and crawled inside my ear, as sometimes happens, and I tried to picture a second head growing from his shoulder. How wondrous it would look! A smile crossed my wind-chapped lips. I saw that I was not mad, and that if some unfortunate destiny were to befall José Gallardo in Tularosa, there would be a wondrous two-headed baby abandoned to the fates, in need of a protector.

The lead weight of my pistols hung heavy on my belt. To know the future is at once a great and terrible thing.

THE CRYING
OF THE GULLS

Ogilvie had never set foot inside the Mint Club before. In
fact he'd only been in Sheridan, Wyoming, for three days, but
already he felt strongly that he'd come to the right place. Travel,
like whiskey, fires the imagination. Rolling into Sheridan with a
backseat full of empty bottles, Ogilvie had pulled off the highway on a hunch. He'd been driving west the way some people
leap screaming from bridges and high windows. This of course
is an American tradition. His last stop on the way out had been
in Spearfish, on the South Dakota border, where he'd gotten

soused in a doublewide bar called the Sod House. In a room full of strangers Ogilvie had raised his voice to say things he could no longer recall, things that would have been provocative and unpleasant. He remembered the big Indian hitting him, once. He woke up behind the wheel of his Oldsmobile somewhere on the edge of town with a swollen cheek and dry blood clotted in the fine hairs of his nose. The clean dawn light on sagebrush prairie, long shadows from lonesome trees, the ferric taste of blood in his mouth—all of this had stirred Ogilvie deeply. Boundaries seemed to be giving way; this was the frontier, where anything could happen. Inside the Mint Club three nights later, a woman at the bar turned as he pushed through the swinging doors. She appeared to recognize him at once—though of course he was a total stranger—and nothing could have surprised Ogilvie less. "It's you," she said. "I never thought I'd see *you* again."

Ogilvie smiled. The neon beer signs cast a dusky glow upon the room. "Take a good look," he said. "I'm back."

Only three days in Sheridan but so far Ogilvie liked it. He'd rented a studio apartment that afternoon and spent the evening out in front of his building, relaxing in a lawn chair with a Solo cup of Evan Williams. Teenagers in domestic trucks cruised back and forth on Big Horn Avenue. They whistled and cat-called to each other, boys taunting girls, boys taunting boys. Later there would be awkward sex and fistfights, beery love and violence, reconciliations, broken promises. It was Friday night. On the rise just north of downtown the clan of municipal buffalo threw buffalo-shaped silhouettes against the darkening sky in their hilltop enclosure. Families strolled up the hill to greet them, buffalo-loving children leading the way, excited. The animals would be musky, dusty, wise-eyed, rolling in their own chips. The late-setting August sun had cracked like the yolk of an egg over easy, bleeding its colors hither and yon. All around the town the land was lying open and immense. Ogilvie had headed west to find the west and now he knew he'd found it. Here it was.

Back in the Mint Club, the woman he did not know returned his smile. "You've got a lot of nerve," she said.

"And that's not all. What are you drinking?"

"Same as always."

"Make it two then." He signaled the bartender, pointing at the woman's empty glass and holding up two fingers.

She bit her lip. "A lot of nerve," she said again, pronouncing the last word in two parts: *nuh-erve*. She repeated it this way several times, drumming a tune with her palms on the scarred oak bar. Then she picked up her glass and held it against her ear. "I think I hear the ocean."

She was tall — taller than Ogilvie — and rawboned thin in a tank top that was stained down the front, possibly bloodied. Her pale face was made of sharp angles and the eyes bulged out too much but she was pretty. Some women wear hard living like a carnation in their hair. Their drinks arrived.

"Bottoms up," said Ogilvie.

"The best way." She leaned in close, breathing heat in his ear. "Jesus, I'm lit," she whispered. "You can't imagine how fucking lit I am."

"I can imagine." He took a sip from his glass. Tequila.

"*Imagine*," she said. "Of all the nights for you to show up."

"You always said I had great timing."

"Did I?" She laughed—head back, mouth open. No one laughs like that in the winter, Ogilvie thought. She extended a finger and placed it on the tip of his nose. "I'm thinking of a number between one and a hundred."

Ogilvie considered her bug-like eyes. They looked ready to fall out of her head any minute now. He could picture them rolling off down the bar, dropping to the sawdusted floor, exploding. Her finger, tapping out a secret rhythm on the end of his nose, seemed to be imparting knowledge. "Seventy-three," he said.

She mouthed the word *Bingo.*

They emptied their glasses. Ogilvie signaled the bartender again.

The woman leaned back on her stool. She stared up at the ceiling, waggling her head slowly back and forth. "So where you been then, cowboy?" She laughed again. "Thin ben, bow coy."

Ogilvie narrowed his eyes. Once, in Chicago, a female bus driver had mistaken him for a man named Terrence. *No way, Terrence,* she shouted down from her seat behind the big wheel. *You're not getting on my bus.* This was many years ago. "Chicago," Ogilvie said.

"Well, good for you. Mrs. O'Leary's cow and all that. Things have gotten worse around here though—a lot worse." She leaned forward and looked at him significantly. "You wouldn't believe it."

"Try me."

"Oh, don't worry," she said. "I'll try you."

[12]

She raised her eyebrows and her drink. Ogilvie touched his glass to hers.

"Here's to good things going bad," she said.

They tossed off the tequila and she threw her glass against the wall. It shattered almost musically, like wind chimes in a hurricane. Everyone in the Mint Club turned to look.

"All right, Virginia," said the bartender. He was coming at them slowly, wiping his hands on a rag. "I think you've had about enough." Then, to Ogilvie: "She's been here since two o'clock."

They walked to Ogilvie's car laughing. He couldn't remember what they were laughing about. "Just like old times," Virginia said.

"I don't remember where you live," said Ogilvie. He jabbed at the keyhole on his door and missed, then missed again.

They got in the Oldsmobile and she told him the way. Then she got quiet for a long time. They were traveling a road that was new to Ogilvie. It led them out of town to the west; the streetlights trailed off. Fortunately, the road ran arrow straight. The night was moonless but Ogilvie could feel miles of empty space pressing in on them from either side of the blacktop. It just goes on forever, he thought.

"I don't know who you are," Virginia said after a while. Her voice was calm. Gone was its charming, boozy lilt.

"I guess not."

"I've never seen you before in my life."

Ogilvie did not respond.

"I thought you were somebody else," she said, almost offhandedly.

"My name is Sam Ogilvie."

Virginia said nothing. She was looking out the window and Ogilvie wasn't sure she'd heard him. He could see the ghost of her face, lit pale green by the dashboard instruments, traveling across the framed black void.

"Not much out there," he said.

"Oh," said Virginia, "there's plenty." She spread her hand flat against the glass. "My father believes this land is haunted."

Ogilvie turned his eyes from the road for a moment, trusting the car's alignment. "Haunted by who?"

"By the Talking People."

He nodded. The Talking People. "Who are the Talking People?"

"Not everyone hears them. Daddy doesn't hear them."

"Do you hear them?"

"My mother heard them."

Ogilvie faced forward again. The road flowed out of the night and fell beneath the tires with a high-pitched hum. "And what did they say? To your mother?"

"All kinds of things."

"Like what?"

"They told her to go outside," Virginia said. "They told her to walk out and be with them in the field behind our house."

"That's not so bad."

"This was in the winter — February, forty below. She was

home by herself and walked out with no coat on and sat down in the snow. Daddy found her when he came home."

Ogilvie tightened his grip on the steering wheel. He could see the white of his knuckles in the weak dashboard glow. "She was dead?"

Virginia didn't answer. She turned on the radio. Static. The antenna was broken. She turned it off.

"But who are they?" Ogilvie asked.

Virginia laughed. "Who are you, Sam Ogilvie?"

Ogilvie felt himself smile. "Who are you, Virginia what's-your-name?"

"I'm the girl in trouble."

"What kind of trouble?"

"Bad trouble. Money trouble. Trunny mubble." She had a fine, stony, bitter laugh. It went with her face. She put a hand on Ogilvie's knee. "Trad bunny mubble."

Ogilvie covered her hand with his own. "That's no real trouble at all."

She turned up her palm, tangling their fingers. "You must be rich, Sam Ogilvie."

"I have $162 in a Ziploc bag in my toilet tank."

She lived in a wooden farmhouse, two stories with a broad porch across the front. There was a light on inside and no other lights could be seen in any direction. They were alone in a vast black sea. Ogilvie watched her walk ahead of him across the dead summer grass in the dim yard. Her long body seemed to sway in the breeze murmuring down from someplace further west. He paused on the porch steps to listen. The wind brushed over him, worrying the edges of his hair. Its sound whispered softly in his ears.

Virginia had opened the front door. She leaned against the frame. The hall light made a silhouette of her form. "Are you coming?" she asked.

In the morning Ogilvie awoke to the repeating beep of a truck in reverse. Virginia was no longer in the bed but the smell of maple syrup wafted up from the kitchen. He stood naked and went to the window. The window looked out from the back of the house. There were maybe forty yards of open grass and then a chain-link fence topped with razor wire. Beyond the fence a strip mine was in operation. A canyon had been dug into the earth and a dump truck was climbing toward its rim on a graded road, loaded with some type of rock. Ogilvie put his pants on.

"Virginia," he called as he came down the stairs. At the bottom he turned left, following the smell through the dining room. "Virginia."

The kitchen was bright with morning sun. A small man stood at the stove, pouring circles of pancake batter from a pitcher into a cast-iron skillet. He was elderly, maybe in his seventies, but handled the pitcher with confidence—perhaps even with flair. He wore twill pants held up by suspenders that crisscrossed at the back of a red flannel shirt. The clothes fit him loosely; he had probably been larger once. His face as he turned to look at Ogilvie was somehow the face of a larger man. It had the presence of size, staring at Ogilvie through narrowed eyes across the kitchen. "Virginia is not here," the man said.

"Oh," said Ogilvie.

There was a small breakfast table by the window and at this table sat a woman in a wheelchair. The woman's head was tilted at a slight angle. Her claw-like hands held the chair's armrests in a palsied grip.

"I'm Lawrence Clover," the man said, "Virginia's father. My daughter has gone to work but instructed us to offer you a breakfast." He smiled but his smile was not warm. "Sam."

"Thanks. But I should get to work myself," Ogilvie explained, though he hadn't had a job in months. The feeling of work had left him entirely. He was a free agent.

Clover walked over and stood behind the wheelchair, resting his hands on the woman's shoulders. "This is my wife, Corrine. She suffered a brain damage some years ago. Corrine doesn't speak but she can see and hear you."

Ogilvie said, "Hello, Corrine."

Clover told him to sit down.

Ogilvie smiled. The truth was that he felt pretty good, at least by his own standards. He'd sweated out most of the alcohol in bed with Virginia and was barely hungover at all. He inhaled deeply, breathing in the smells of syrup and cooking batter. He was very hungry. "Well, I suppose just for a minute. Hate to work on an empty stomach."

He took the chair to Corrine's left, nodding to her as he sat. She looked to be past middle age but not as old as Clover, though it was hard to tell exactly. Her mouth hung open, the tongue performing lazy, aimless movements inside. She wore a floral print dress. Her body seemed bloated and emaciated at the same time. Her eyes wandered over to Ogilvie and then wandered away. She had a drop of syrup on her chin. Ogilvie turned and looked out the window. "That's a hell of a mine."

Clover made a noise in his throat, something akin to a growl, and walked back to the stove. "There's nothing they won't do to wring money from this land." Wielding a metal spatula, he flipped the sizzling pancakes with a series of violent wrist-flicks.

"I suppose not."

Clover transferred the pancakes to a plate, brought them over and set them in front of Ogilvie, then sat down himself across the table. Narrowing his eyes again, he stared out the window toward the fence and the mine beyond. The deep lines on his face trapped shadows in a map-like latticework. He said, "They won't stop till all of Wyoming's one big hole in the ground."

The pancakes were delicious. Ogilvie realized that there had been no dinner the night before. There was no point in denying that dinner was a meal he missed from time to time, a meal that had a way of getting lost. The pancakes seemed temporarily to dispel the notion of evil in the world. "I'm sure it'll never go that far," he mumbled through a syrup-soaked mouthful.

"The hell you say."

"What are they mining, anyway?"

"Kitty litter."

"Excuse me?"

Clover slammed right fist into left palm with startling force. A muscle twitched in his cheek. "The bastards are mining kitty litter."

Ogilvie glanced over at Corrine. Her lazy eyes had been on him but darted away when he looked — or so he thought.

"I didn't know they mined for that."

"A special kind of clay," Clover told him. "The geologists say there's a fortune of it under my house." He turned from the window, sunlight sliding off the front of his face, and fixed his raptor stare on Ogilvie once more. "You wouldn't believe what they've offered for this place."

Ogilvie leaned in. "But you're not selling?"

"That's right," Clover said. He raised a gnarled finger, a finger like a piece of scrap iron, and pointed it across the table. "I won't sell for a truckload of their pagan gold."

Pagan gold—Ogilvie felt giddy. The Great West was like a natural preservative for these Old Testament types. Clover had probably wrestled bears for the pleasure of smelling death on their fur. His righteousness was forged in blood. There was a trace of the same frontier violence in Virginia's reckless way with drink, and her cornered-badger style of "making love." Ogilvie knew that a network of deep scratches like whiplashes had been carved into his back the night before. She had branded him like a head of cattle; even now the bare scrapings of his skin would be there underneath her fingernails, wherever she was. "Fuck 'em," he said to Clover.

Clover nodded in agreement, but slowly, with the indifference of shrewd appraisal. "Yes," he said. "Fuck 'em. They who shall see the land rent for shitting cats." He stood, clearing Ogilvie's pancakeless, syrup-smeared plate.

"Wonderful breakfast," Ogilvie said.

Clover did not answer. He went to the sink and stood there with his back to the table. Ogilvie looked out the window again. A dump truck approached the edge of the mine, throwing a haze of dust up behind it, then dipped its nose and disappeared down into the pit. A row of framed photographs lined the windowsill. Virginias of every age smiled out from under glass. She had a thin arm draped across her father's broad shoulders in several of the pictures, and these confirmed that Clover had once been an imposing man with a face like the side of a mountain. Corrine did not appear in any of them. Even as a young girl, Ogilvie saw, Virginia's grin had been dark and cunning. One small shot in particular caught his eye: teenage Virginia, dark hair chopped short and bobbed, driving a knife into the flesh of a rectangular birthday cake. The knife seemed much too big for the job; it was practically a machete, the kind of tool with which Crazy Horse might have smote a pack of wolves. Her face was gleeful, but it was the glee of death and power. Blocky frosting letters on the cake spelled out *Happy Birthday Sharon.*

He picked the frame up to look more closely and then, on an impulse, slipped it into his pocket. Clover was still at the sink with his back turned. Corrine, however, was staring at Ogilvie again, her head bobbing slightly as if in some attempt to protest. Ogilvie saw that her eyes protruded buggishly, not unlike Virginia's. He winked at her and stood from the table.

"Thanks so much for the food," he said loudly, patting his pancake-filled stomach with both hands. "I guess I'd better get on to work now."

August became September and Ogilvie did not see Virginia again. Sometimes he would wander down to the Mint Club, unsure if he was looking for her. In any case she was never there. But in general his situation seemed to be stabilizing, possibly even improving. He ran out of money and had to take work as a line cook at a diner by the interstate. He found, to his surprise, that he liked this job. The waitresses fascinated him. They were old, competent, tough, possessed for the most part of fabulous memories. They were waitresses in the way Ogilvie's father had been Army: it was in their carriage, how they spoke and applied eye shadow, the cigarettes they smoked. Plainly they were members of a tribe; as such they expressed a certain human potential for belonging. Ogilvie took heart in this. They shouted at him in mentholated gravel voices. They shouted orders and Ogilvie produced the food. He drank less. He could feel his life slowing down and the feeling pleased him.

But it was true that he often mistook unknown women for Virginia on the street, through store windows, riding bicycles around town. There were repeated false alarms. Once, crossing the creek that ran under Big Horn Avenue, he caught sight of a lone figure floating away downstream aboard an inner tube. Long brown hair, not unlike Virginia's, spilled over the tube's rubber stern. The woman's hands trailed in the water on either side of her at the end of lean, white arms. She did not turn around. Ogilvie stood watching at the bridge rail until the current ferried her around a bend. The next day he went to the Humane Society and adopted a cat.

The cat was orange and had sagging bunches of loose skin around its belly, which the woman at the Humane Society said was a result of being spayed. This meant that the cat had once been someone else's pet. It was a used cat. Ogilvie liked the cat well enough but decided not to name her, just in case. Still, when he sat outside his building in the evenings—with a beer now, or sometimes even coffee—he would bring the cat out with him and watch her slink around in the tall weeds at the edge of the vacant lot next door. She was sleek, agile, out for mice and voles, the classic picture of a huntress, slack flesh notwithstanding. Watching her, Ogilvie experienced a feeling very much like pride. The cat would come to his windowsill when she wanted to be let back in at night and often they watched TV "together." She learned to do her business outside; Ogilvie did not keep a litter box.

But September wore on. The fall was coming and no one could stop it. In the mornings, at dusk, a change of season in the air: you felt it first at the edges of your body, in your fingertips and the end of your nose. The days remained warm. The prairie grasses turned a deeper yellow. The municipal family of buffalo welcomed a new calf and then the calf died suddenly, mysteriously. It happened on a Sunday and children lined the fence pointing at the corpse until it was taken away. Some of them came down the hill crying, shambling past Ogilvie's building, wailing and attempting to talk all at once, as children do. Ogilvie stood at his open window looking out. The sorrowful noise seemed to reach him from across a great distance, but with urgency. It seemed to contain important news.

A few days later Ogilvie walked on the narrow path beside the creek that crossed Big Horn Avenue. The water babbled as it ran across the stones. Ogilvie closed his eyes and listened. He sensed that there was an idea in the sound, though he could not make the idea out. But the shape of the thing was there and the experience of perceiving this shape was altogether new to Ogilvie; it struck him with the force of discovery.

That afternoon he watched a diced green pepper sizzle on his grill. He added tomato, added onion. He mixed them together with his spatula. The topography of vegetables, tri-colored, spelled out a word or made a symbol; somehow it signified a concept. The concept eluded him, but he knew it was real. He cracked three eggs into a bowl and saw a face in them. The face was not human. It wasn't even a face, really, but more the notion of a face.

He beat the eggs together and it disappeared.

This development was troubling. A communication seemed to be taking place, or an attempted communication — but attempted by whom and to what purpose? The substance of the messages continued to inhabit the dim regions just beyond his grasp, but Ogilvie suspected the work of dark forces. Whether internal or external he couldn't say. The messages would seem at times to be everywhere, and then might disappear for a day, for two days. When they returned he would greet their return with profoundly mixed feelings. This went on for several weeks before the mutilation of his cat.

A drowsy, elegant afternoon early in October: sun-drenched, Indian summer. Ogilvie had worked the lunch shift. When he returned home the cat was lying on the lawn in front of his building, her body stretched out as if to sunbathe. She was missing her left front leg. Seeing Ogilvie, she let out a plaintive whine. The sound was broken into parts, like voices on a cell phone with poor reception, as if some kind of fluid were pooling in the cat's small lungs. Ogilvie dropped to a knee and examined the wound. It was jagged and sticky, the blood having already congealed. A crimson pool of it stained the grass, which meant that the cat had been there for a while, not ten feet from the sidewalk. Pedestrians had passed by and done nothing. They had seen his cat, less one leg and bleeding, and simply continued on their way. Ogilvie looked around. Even now, a woman on the sidewalk regarded him from underneath a straw sunhat. She was middle-aged, likely the mother of children.

"My cat has lost a leg," Ogilvie told her.

The woman turned her head and kept walking.

Ogilvie stared back down at the cat. He ran a finger very lightly over the place where her limb had been torn away. The glaze of blood, the grains of dirt sticking to it, the strands of muscle and tendon, the protruding length of bone—all of these came together and formed a design. The design was not without meaning.

At the animal hospital, in the waiting room, one other man waited with him. The man held a black dachshund on his lap and the dachshund wore a patch over one eye. Tubular fluorescent ceiling lamps threw a harsh glare down on their silent threesome. The hair on Ogilvie's arms seemed very dark in this light, the skin beneath it very pale. He found the effect unnatural and disturbing.

The cat might well die. Blood loss, trauma, the established shape of Ogilvie's fate. The cat was probably dead already.

A newspaper lay scattered on the end table beside his chair. Ogilvie picked it up and began passing his eyes idly across the words. A headline just below the Page One fold announced that a local man had been killed accidentally in his garage two nights before. The victim's name was Lawrence Clover.

Clover had been crushed by his own pickup truck. Precisely how this happened was unclear. He had apparently raised the truck up on jacks sometime in the evening with the intention of rotating its tires, but then went to bed without completing the task. The truck remained aloft. At around three a.m. he re-entered the garage for unknown reasons, crawled underneath the chassis, and presumably dislodged one of the jacks by mistake. No one heard the truck fall; Clover was killed instantly. His daughter, Virginia, discovered the body several hours later.

Ogilvie read through the article twice. There was no mention of foul play. The county coroner had ruled Clover's death an accident and that was that. The coroner was a professional, a trained expert in modes of mortality. His opinion carried the weight of law. This did not necessarily make it correct.

Ogilvie closed his eyes. Above his head the ceiling lamps crackled and buzzed. The sound seemed to vibrate at the precise frequency of his suspicions. *Trunny mubble, pagan gold.* The pirate-faced dachshund put in with a single, sharp, assenting bark: *Woof, Ogilvie, how right you are.*

"Mr. Ogilvie?"

He opened his eyes. The nurse stood before him. At her side, a raven-haired doctor held the cat in his arms. The cat's eyes were not open.

"She's dead," Ogilvie said.

"No," said the doctor, "she's sleeping. She'll sleep for a while." He smiled broadly. It was a deeply competent expression, the smile of a man who winnowed pet souls.

Ogilvie stood and carefully accepted the cat, her body swaddled babe-like in a white towel. "Thank you," he said.

"It's my job."

The doctor's bearing seemed to reflect belief in science, confidence in the logic of natural order. Ogilvie glanced around the room and lowered his voice. "What do you think happened to her leg?"

The doctor shrugged. "Maybe a coyote?" He had magnificent teeth with which to smile. "Then again, maybe not."

Back at his apartment Ogilvie studied the photograph he'd stolen from Virginia's house. Her adolescent face might well have been the face of a future murderess. She seemed to brandish the knife with preternatural poise. She seemed to project, this little Virginia, the self-assurance of a woman twice her age—a woman who knew full well the depth of her capacities. The light of the camera's flash made a starburst where it reflected off the long blade, the leading edge of which was already tasting Sharon's cake.

"What do you think?" he asked the cat, holding the picture up in front of her.

The cat was groggy, just surfacing from under the sedatives, lying splayed on the bed but short one tool for expressing this posture. Ogilvie watched her come to. She moved her head in strange arcs, snatching at slow-moving, invisible flies. Closing his eyes, he could hear the flies buzzing though he knew they did not exist. They buzzed like the lights at the animal hospital, at the same frequency of agreement.

He stood and went to the window. Sliding the glass open, he heard the voices of prairie bugs and the breeze, the droning whisper of cars on the interstate, the murmur of a television, the sharp *clink* of cup against saucer somewhere. In the dark line of trees on the buffalo hill, in the shapes of larger hills stenciled black against the deep blue sky to the west, even in the mottled moonlight making shadows in the alley on the other side of Big Horn Avenue, there was a presence. The presence conveyed invitation. It seemed to be calling Ogilvie out. He might find friends out there, the easy kinship of light and sound.

There was a soft, plosive thump behind him.

Ogilvie turned. The cat had gotten down off the bed—though he didn't see how—and was trying to walk on her remaining legs. Awkwardly she gathered herself and stood, but when she dared a step her balance collapsed and she pitched forward onto her bandaged stump. *Thump*. The dull thud was like a gunshot in some underwater dream, aquamen firing muskets at fierce narwhals. The cat was growing confused, alarmed. She did not understand where her leg had gone. Neither did Ogilvie. She became increasingly frantic, almost trying to run in circles on the floor. On the floorboards her stump went *thump, thump, thump. Thump, thump, thump* went her stump. The unrhythmic rhythm seemed to be in some kind of communication with the presence outside. Ogilvie watched the cat in horror, as she seemed

[27]

to be watching herself, flopping around the room like an epileptic's marionette. He picked up Virginia's picture, searched it again for a clue. He faced the window—the strange geometries of shadow outside, the dark shapes and speaking noises. The wind turned and came through the screen. It touched his face, drying his eyeballs and the spit on his teeth.

The kitty litter mine had not stopped work for Lawrence Clover's funeral. A high white sun sharpened the din of motors and shouts and pneumatic drills drifting across the broad valley as the Clover house gathered black-clad mourners in. The industrial racket seemed somehow to be orchestrating this process of assemblage. The funeral-goers floated from their cars, some clutching flowers at their sides. Ogilvie leaned on the open door of his Oldsmobile. He wore his only suit—a light, non-funereal blue two-piece—and the bolo tie he'd purchased that very morning at the Junior League thrift store on Burkitt Street. He was no longer sure about the tie. A fine spray of dust like ocean mist hovered over the gaping mine pit and above that, a hawk circling stiff-winged against the pale sky like a stringless kite.

Folding chairs had been arranged in the parlor. Most were occupied by the time Ogilvie entered. He took a seat in the back row. At the head of the room, in front of the fireplace, the coffin stretched out lengthways. It seemed to draw the crowd's silence as a black hole draws light. The front half of the lid had been propped open and Clover's eyes stared up at the ceiling through lids pulled shut by the undertaker. Through a door beside the fireplace Virginia emerged to take her place behind the coffin-side podium. She scanned the audience with her ruthless, protuberant eyes, before settling, Ogilvie thought, on him. He straightened up in his chair. Scarcely a month ago they had held each other naked, Virginia thrashing viciously against him, drawing blood with bared nails.

"My father," she began, "was not a perfect man."

Of course she was radiant. The black dress set off her pale skin. Her height commanded the room. Audaciously, she wore heels. Ogilvie sweated freely. Clover lay still, eulogized like Caesar by his killer, dispatched after a lifetime of rugged western manliness by his own daughter for kitty litter blood money. Maybe. Virginia's composure was captivating. She seemed flawless in her eloquence, though Ogilvie had almost immediately lost track of what she was saying. His desire for her was pressing but complex; he needed something from her but wasn't quite sure what. He alone might know her secret. Corrine might know too, but she did not appear to be in the audience. He looked all around; she wasn't there. It occurred to him that she must also have been done away with somehow, likely shipped off to some ghastly state-run sanitarium where the orderlies were all sex offenders and the sheets were never changed.

At the reception, in the long dining room, somber guests lined up to express their regrets to Virginia. Ogilvie hung back at the refreshment table, anxiously stuffing his face with French pastries. Fortunately, there was also a makeshift bar. He stood with bourbon and éclair, staring at the lunchmeat tray. The variously colored meats, fanned out in a broad arc, seemed to comprise a sign of warning. The meats sought to dissuade him but Ogilvie would not be swayed. Virginia presently worked her way through the receiving line; the crowd drifted away and left her alone in the center of the room. Ogilvie sauntered boldly over, craning to peck her proffered cheek.

"Sam," she said, "it's so good of you to come."

"Yes, long time no see."

"Sorry I haven't called. Things have been difficult."

"That's OK, I never gave you my number."

"Well maybe you'll give it to me now."

"I don't have a phone."

She smiled. "How odd."

Ogilvie smiled back. "In any event, I'm terribly sorry." He threw her a sly wink. "For your loss, I mean."

"Thanks. Did you just wink at me?"

"Of course not." He glanced around the room. "So, how long will you wait to sell this place?"

"I don't know," Virginia said. "I hadn't really planned on selling at all. Doubt it's worth anything with that mine next door." She gestured vaguely out the window.

Ogilvie followed the gesture with his eyes. The sun had started sinking, brushing the rising mine dust with shades of gold. He leaned in close and whispered, "That's not what your father told me."

Virginia laughed gently. "Did he try to sell you that old line?" She put her hand on Ogilvie's shoulder. "I'm afraid my dad entertained a few delusions late in life. He wasn't quite all there. There's no kitty litter under this house, if that's what he told you—if there were, he would've sold the place himself a long time ago. I know he wanted to after my mom died."

Ogilvie nodded. "Ah yes, your mother."

Virginia cocked her head to the side.

"Your dearly departed mother."

She took her hand off his shoulder and sniffed the air. "Have you been drinking, Sam?"

"Yes. But tell me something: why set a truck up on jacks and then just walk away from it, go to bed, leave it like that?"

"Maybe he got tired. Maybe the phone rang. Obviously we're not going to talk about this."

"You weren't here?"

"I was in my room."

"And why, even if he had left it that way, would an old man go crawling around underneath a jacked-up truck at three o'clock in the morning?" He lifted his eyebrows and inclined his head toward her a few more inches.

Virginia studied him briefly and retrieved her smile. "I think he was looking for the cat. The cat usually sleeps in the house, but she was in the garage when I found him. Really, Sam, I can't tell you how charming this is."

"I see. The cat."

She crossed her arms in front of her chest. "What are you getting at, Sherlock?"

Ogilvie winked again. "Nothing special."

"Brilliant. Tell me something: was it a crew of goons from the mining company, or did I kill him myself?"

"Maybe *you* should tell *me*."

"Maybe you should go."

"Don't worry," Ogilvie whispered, "I'm not going to turn you in. That's not what this is about."

"What a relief. That's a nice suit, by the way — those string ties just melt me. You look like an extra on *Dallas*." She pointed to the door. "Please leave."

Ogilvie mopped his brow. He could sense the room's attention shifting toward them, people putting down coffee cups and brioches to listen. "But I haven't passed along my condolences to you mother."

"My *mother*," Virginia hissed, "is quite fucking dead. I don't care what my dad told you — he was a senile old bastard. He lost it. I don't know why the hell he crawled under that trucking fuck, I mean fucking truck." Like her late father, she had a muscle in her cheek that became active when she was upset.

Ogilvie lowered his eyes. He tried briefly to sort through these claims. "But I met her," he said.

"Excuse me?"

"I met her — Corrine. We met."

"Is this a joke, Sam? Is this some kind of sick fucking joke? I'm sorry I never called you. My mother is dead. Get out of here."

Everyone was staring now, though for some reason nobody approached to intervene. "She was in a wheelchair, at the breakfast table —" Ogilvie mimed the arm motions of a wheelchair athlete.

"You're crazy," Virginia said. "Please go."

Ogilvie looked down at his finely polished shoes. But he *had* met Corrine. Certainly he seemed to have met Corrine. A silence developed. Finally he put his lips very close to Virginia's ear and she did not move away. "I hear them," he breathed.

"Hear who?" she breathed back.

"The Talking People."

Now she moved away. "Jesus," she whispered.

"I know."

"Sam, there are no Talking People. That's just an old Indian story, frontier voodoo."

"But what about your mother?"

"God, I was so drunk—I don't even know why I told it to you."

"No." Ogilvie shook his head. "I hear them, I see them. They're Talking to me."

"Listen to yourself, Sam. There are no Talking People. You need help."

"What about your mother?"

"My mother wasn't a happy person. My father didn't treat her well." She spoke evenly but her big eyes seemed wild, as they had the night she and Ogilvie met. "They're in your head, Sam. You have to get help."

Ogilvie bit his lip. He could feel the color burning in his cheeks, its heat like a noise in his brain. The assembled faces continued to stare, disapproving—the stern women, the men not unlike Clover himself with their rough-hewn features and horse-back posture. Ogilvie began to mumble a muddled apology to his shiny feet. Then he stopped and looked back up at Virginia. "I should probably go," he said.

"Yes," she agreed, "you probably should."

Outside, the mine had fallen silent. No trucks rumbled; the miners had gone home. Ogilvie fingered the dual strings of his new used tie. He could see her point—about the tie, about his being insane. Certainly he'd considered these possibilities himself. A bank of tufted clouds drifted down from the north. They were very high, as clouds in Wyoming always seemed to be, and gazing down the parched grass valley Ogilvie could see the twisted shapes of their long shadows lying scattered on the land. He sat down on the hood of his car and studied the physical relationships: cloud, sun, shadow, earth. The evening crickets were beginning to chirp. They had plenty to say, but that didn't mean you had to listen. Somewhere in the sky he could hear the drone of an airplane passing high over the empty, lonesome country, over the territory of cattle drives and massacred Indians, over the bones of nameless cowboys returning into dust.

Three years passed. Ogilvie drifted west with his crippled cat: Tacoma, Sacramento, Los Angeles. There were ups and downs, but for the most part he managed to live quietly. Taking limited exercise, the cat became obese; Ogilvie, however, began jogging. He watched less television and read more books. He learned to play guitar. Sometimes he would strum a little tune for the cat and sing to her: James Taylor, Cat Stevens. Then in L.A. he met a woman named Meg. Ogilvie was driving a school bus at the time; Meg's teenage son was among his daily passengers. Meg had gotten pregnant in the pool house at a party in Topanga Canyon when she was nineteen. This was during her long and prolific drug phase. The father was a B-list TV star. Like Ogilvie, Meg regarded herself as someone with a deep capacity for trouble. Like Ogilvie, she was trying to embrace a more peaceful existence. They played cribbage together, cooked good meals, attended her son's roller hockey games.

"We've earned the right to be boring," Meg liked to say.

The wedding was at the Bel Air Hotel on a fine day in March. Meg's family was in the industry; they owned a graphics company that specialized in movie posters—a niche market, quite lucrative. The band wore white tuxedos. Richard Dreyfus gave an amusing toast. Meg's father took Ogilvie aside at the reception and offered to bring him into the company as a vice-president, a position for which he had absolutely no qualifications. Luckily, none were necessary. It was mostly a people job. Ogilvie played golf and talked on the phone a great deal. He surprised himself by proving to be a nimble schmoozer—so nimble in fact that he was sent to France the following spring to represent the company at Cannes.

Ah, spring on the Riviera.

Cannes, of course, was a disaster during the festival. Ogilvie had never seen so many attractive people snorting cocaine naked until sunrise on yachts. Men rode jet skis heroically in the moonlight; on deck, beautiful women gave head in the shadows. There was a lot of talk. Everybody wanted to be taken seriously. On the schooner of an Italian paper magnate, in the bathroom line, a Swiss model told Ogilvie that she had seen Brando's cock in a sauna on Majorca, that it was huge, that she was considering Buddhism.

Each night Ogilvie returned to his room at some terrible hour and called Meg in California so they could laugh at what he'd seen, and possibly have phone sex. Each morning he rose before lunch and went for a brisk walk by himself along the esplanade: the sleek boats bobbing gently on the harbor swell, pastel water, condoms and champagne glasses washing up on the beach. He'd never felt better in his life. That year's Palme d'Or went to an independent French film, *The Crying of the Gulls*, and many were hailing its director, Orenbuch, as a man of genius. Ogilvie was sitting at the Majestic Barrière bar on the last night of the festival with a Parisian critic named Rondeaux when Orenbuch entered to a standing ovation. He waved grandly to the crowd—a tallish, pleasant-looking Frenchman with a ring of dark curls around his otherwise bald head. His tuxedo was rumpled; he seemed to have kind eyes. The woman on his arm was equally tall. In fact, it was Virginia Clover.

"Merci!" Orenbuch shouted. "Thank you all!"

Ogilvie nearly laughed out loud. She looked marvelous, far better than before. Her thin face had filled out just enough, its color gone to honey from the sun. The flush of her cheeks seemed instantly, transparently, to convey the benefits of healthful living—of fresh fruit, languorous sex, and expensive wine, possibly all at once. Ogilvie nudged Rondeaux. "Who is that woman?"

"That?" Rondeaux sneered. "That is Orenbuch's wife— an American."

"She's beautiful, don't you think?"

"Bah, they are all beautiful." He spat on the bar. "Where will beauty get you? She has something else, this one." He cupped his hand around Ogilvie's ear and murmured, "She is *rich*."

"Rich?"

"Yes, rich, rich. Where do you think Orenbuch gets money for his sham of a movie? She pays for it all, she bankrolled.

Yes, she bankrolled him."

"But where does her money come from?"

"His farce of a film. Melodramatic nonsense, violins and nudity. That dolphin dying in slow motion—I threw up in my mouth."

"Do you know where?"

Rondeaux threw his hands in the air. "Where? Where? She is American. She sits on the toilet and dollars fall from her ass, no? Where does your money come from, eh Ogilvie?"

"Me?" Ogilvie grinned. "I married it."

Rondeaux grinned back. "Ah, then you are smart." He reached into his breast pocket and produced a crumpled pack of Turkish cigarettes. "Very smart, for an American."

Virginia had not seen him. He did not seek her attention. Her bearing was regal. Orenbuch seemed to have stepped back: Virginia, front and center, blowing kisses to the crowd. She wore their applause like a garland of roses. "Bravo," Ogilvie whispered. He joined in the clapping until it died away.

"Yes," Rondeaux said, "it is a good reason—as good as any, at least. Me, I married for love. Do you have a match?"

Ogilvie did not have a match.

Rondeaux smiled around the unlit cigarette. He was a small man but dirty in a way small men usually aren't: yellow teeth, greasy hair, a wispy mustache. His jacket was frayed at the sleeve. "A poor girl, both of us were poor, from a small town outside Lyon. We came to Paris with nothing but we were young, we didn't know any better. We were very happy. Fucking all night—she was exquisite, we barely slept. You can imagine. Across the hall from our apartment was a man with no legs. I do not know how he lost them. An auto wreck, maybe, or a tiger bit them off. Of course you do not ask these things. He went around the city in a wheelchair but in his home he would not use the chair. It was a filthy building and all the first floor apartments had pipes across the ceiling, dozens of them in every direction. So our friend, he hangs rope all through these pipes—like a spider web, see? Ropes from every part of the ceiling. And he swings around his house like a monkey on these ropes. Much easier than the chair, he says. You should see his arms from doing this—like a Russian gymnast. A very charming man, my wife and I both liked him very much. He knew card tricks, sleight of hand. A good storyteller. At first he comes over for dinner once a week, then mabe twice. Soon he is traveling with us on holiday to Normandy. But I liked him very much, you see. We both did." Rondeaux looked up from his glass. His mustache was uneven, Ogilvie noticed, a little longer on the right side than the left. Orenbuch and Virginia had been shown to a table in the corner overlooking the harbor. The two of them were laughing about something now, their heads very close together. Rondeaux laughed too. "Well, you can see where this story is going. It is all a mystery, eh Ogilvie? Let us have another drink, on your wife."

CRUELTY TO ANIMALS

I am sitting in the recreation lounge at Dr. _____'s, which frankly seems unable to decide whether it wants to be a drying out facility or a loony bin. We have drinkers here, drug abusers, mental cases — I suppose this is a place that does not discriminate among the well off and disturbed. The brochure calls it a "wellness retreat," which I find to be a lovely anachronism, and recalls for me a simpler time when crazy Aunt Agnes was sent to the country to recover from her exhaustion and nobody ever talked about her again. Back in Westchester County I'm sure they are talking. Samantha may be teased about it by her schoolmates, and my wife may already be fed up with the way conversation seems to stop when she enters the locker room at her gym. People have always perplexed me in this way. Gossip seems to hold a bottomless fascination for everyone, but truth—truth is ignored like poor old Agnes, rotting away in leg irons and fear of experimental shock treatments in a sanitarium outside Plattsburgh.

Here things aren't so bad, really. The meals are good, and the pills are better. So many pretty pills: who needs to drink? Oh, it's true that I sometimes try to bribe the orderly for a nip of this or that, but he is a man of integrity, and I ask him mostly in order to admire the gleam of righteousness that flashes in his frost blue eyes. There is a logic to this place that I find appealing, or perhaps more accurately, a willingness to accept the absence of logic; this, in my opinion, is the only irrefutable verity, and people here seem to understand it. Walter Hogan loses a hotly contested point in Ping-Pong, attempts to eat his paddle, and defecates on the table. He is led away and a nurse comes in to dispose of the evidence, but the rest of us have already turned back to the television, where, hilariously, the coyote runs himself off the cliff yet again.

It would be difficult to recount from the beginning the series of events that brought me here, so I will instead start with the finish—with the climax, as it were—which begins in classic fashion with the shrill ring of a telephone. I was sitting in my office on a Tuesday afternoon, picking my cuticles with a pair of chrome tweezers. I lifted the receiver and tucked it into the crook of my shoulder, leaving my hands free for the tweezers. On the far end of the line, in suburban Philadelphia, my brother greeted me with a deep and mournful sigh.

"It's me," Ben said. His voice was like a deflated volleyball. "Rebecca has gone off the deep end."

I sat there nodding, considering the strangeness of his phrase. What do swimming pools really have to do with insanity? No more than nuts, I guess, no more than bananas. The language with its bent logic and bewildering colloquialisms only contributes to the general morass.

"What happened?"

Another sigh. "Off her rocker," Ben said. "She's lost her marbles."

I should not have been surprised. Ben's wife Rebecca is a beautiful woman—in her middle forties she is still a beautiful woman, but with very big eyes, round eyes. The eyes of a lunatic. She was always possessed of a disquieting eccentricity that only seemed to deepen with age. If I were pressed to classify this quality more narrowly, I might describe it as an outsized need for affection—and I don't mean this in the physical sense. Even fifteen years ago she was the kind of woman who imposed herself with untoward intensity on strangers and new acquaintances, monopolizing your college roommate, visiting from California, for the duration of a cocktail party, or holding up the bank line by means of an extended chat with the teller. I suppose this was just her chosen way of expressing loneliness—expressing, that is, a desperation that all of us feel. But the social contract is based largely on the understanding that we should all suffer our desperation in private, so Rebecca made people uncomfortable. The bank teller might be friendly at first, offering the usual banal pleasantries—she is pretty and he is not unkind; customer relations is a part of his job—but once all her checks have been deposited and the balance transfers done, he will begin to cast nervous glances toward the people behind her in line, attempting by way of his expression to communicate the fact that their delay is not his fault, that he too is being victimized, that this lady is a kook.

Of course we are all interested in the vague sorcery of love. To be honest, I think this habit of Rebecca's may have been part of what attracted Ben to her in the first place; I think he may have regarded it as a mark of offbeat charm. Whenever you love somebody, their flaws become a part of it—maybe the leading part, since our flaws are most often what make us unique. And there's no doubt that Ben loved his wife. He went right on loving her, even as her connection to reality became more fickle—as she lost her job at the art museum, lost $6,000 in a pyramid scheme, tried to move a homeless man into their guest room. The catalog of setbacks grew long. He went right on loving her but there had to be certain compromises. Foremost among these was Ben's decision that the two of them should not have children—a wise choice, understandable to everybody except Rebecca. She was enraged with him and stayed that way, off and on, for years. Her heart was broken. She turned to animals.

That someone afflicted by Rebecca's particular strain of neediness should find solace in the affection of pets is not surprising. At first Ben's house gave quarter to a range of the usual domesticated suspects: dogs, cats, birds, a fish now and then. More recently, Rebecca had become taken with the more exotic concept of chinchillas; and not just owning the fluffy vermin, but breeding them as well. I don't know where this idea came from but it was all fine with Ben. He had long since adopted the strategy of humoring his wife's humorable whims, and thus bought for her two plump, not inexpensive chinchillas somehow marked as prime candidates for reproduction (unlike Rebecca). A deluxe, lacquered wood condominium was erected in the study, and, like drunken adolescents locked together in a closet by their giggling friends, the chichillas promptly surrendered to nature's tender impulse. However, as with most teenage romances, the end proved to be less than storybook when Rebecca, in the grip of what fevered emotions I can only guess, seized the pregnant mother, placed her in the dryer, and set the machine to run a full, deadly cycle. Permanent press was never more permanent than that fateful afternoon. It was this last set of events that Ben had called to relate.

I sat with the receiver against my ear, trying to imagine the incident from a number of viewpoints. There was that of Aristotle, the male chinchilla, but science claims that animals are not subject to the human instincts toward monogamy, domestic family relations, and romantic love. Still, it's hard to believe that Aristotle's mind could have been haunted by no trace of anthropomorphic sorrow when night fell and his woman had yet to come home. There was that of Maude, the female chinchilla, and I wondered exactly how long it had taken her to realize that she wasn't headed to the living room couch for another episode of *General Hospital*, as per usual on weekday afternoons. There was Rebecca's perspective to consider, but the governing forces of such a mind are probably impossible to grasp. And although it was Ben who described the episode to me, I still find it difficult to comprehend what my brother's precise thoughts might have been when he entered the laundry room that evening to discover the fur, the blood, the fetid stench of a dead rodent at high temperature, and his lovely, large-eyed wife slumped against the washing machine in tears.

"I've had it," he said. "Jesus, Stevie, I'm finished," though from his grim, soldierly tone of resignation, I knew that Ben would keep going. I could tell that he would just go on and on.

"What can I do to help?"

"Not a thing, little brother. There's nothing anyone can do."

Well, yes. Obviously an account of this nature would be disturbing under any circumstance, but its resonance was deepened for me by an ominous sense of parallel: it was a story that suggested the shape of anxieties already cluttering my head. Hanging up the phone, I rose from my chair and began pacing the length of the movie screen window that stretched out behind my desk. Beyond the glass New York City seemed to be going drowsily about its business, as it will always appear to do from forty-nine stories in the air, though we know from the morning paper that every day children are raped, the handicapped are mugged, and widows are swindled in confidence games. I suddenly remembered something Rebecca had told me at Thanksgiving: that chinchillas, like the gremlins of Hollywood, should not be gotten wet, and that they bathed by rolling in a special type of ultra-fine dust that had to be ordered through the mail. These facts now seemed depressing, even vulgar. Observing the glacial pile of tedium menacing me from my desk with its slow, inevitable force, the pleasant notion of stepping out for a drink entered my mind. I was just arriving at that place in middle age where a man begins to reevaluate his well-learned habits of self-denial; life, after all, is not so long as we imagine in our youth. I decided to give myself the afternoon off.

Emerging from my office, I informed my secretary that I would be leaving to keep a doctor's appointment, and there was an awkward silence as we each considered the poor quality of this lie. Nora glanced from the clock to my empty schedule and back to me. "The doctor, Mr. Kerwood?"

"Yes, that's right," I said, arching my eyebrows. "The doctor."

"You didn't tell me about any doctor."

"Well, silly me." I smiled. "It must have slipped my mind."

"What kind of doctor?"

I paused. "Prostate," I said. "The prostate doctor." I mimed the medic's inquisitive fingers and gave Nora solemn nod.

She tapped her own fingers on the top of her desk and pursed her thin, colorless lips in a look of troubled skepticism. "You should tell me about these things in advance," she said. "That would help me."

"Well, OK." I broadened my smile, but distress still lingered in her face. Nora was not an insolent woman—quite the opposite, actually—but she had no doubt taken note of a certain deterioration in my work habits over the preceding days, weeks, months; I had lost precise track. She was concerned. Her concern was a nuisance, but also poignant. "Don't worry," I explained. "It's nothing serious. Just a check-up."

"What about your three o'clock?"

"Have Merriwether handle it."

"And your other calls?"

"Forget the calls," I told her. "In fact, you may go home. You deserve a rest, Nora, a little extra time for yourself and whatnot." I wanted to tell Nora other things too: that there was nothing for her to worry about, that human resources would find her another place in the firm as soon as I was gone. She had been working beneath me for nearly a year, and was almost striking in her plainness, if such is possible. Her absence of chin had crossed some never-to-be-crossed line, her breasts barely dented the inside of her blouse. I wanted to tell Nora that I would take her dancing sometime, take her out in a rowboat on the lake in Central Park, or maybe share with her a root beer float.

"Are you sure, Mr. Kerwood?"

"Sure I'm sure," I assured her, tossing off a jaunty wink that would no doubt receive its own giddy paragraph in her journal. "I'll see you tomorrow."

But of course, none of us are promised tomorrow. It was really just a matter of time, I knew, before the axe succumbed to gravity. If not for my fourteen years of faithful service to the firm, if not for the handful of sales records still in my unchallenged possession, I would no doubt have been called to the carpet already for my performance, or rather my escalating failure to perform. People around the office were whispering; they didn't understand the change that had come over me, and frankly I would have struggled to explain it myself. A man wakes up one morning, looks in the mirror, sees a face he no longer recog-nizes—stop me if you've heard this one. For me it was something different, something less precise but more profound, an external incoherence that had come to weigh on my mind with increasing force.

Stepping out of my building into the warm spring air on Third Avenue, I felt a little better right away. I pulled a deep breath down into my lungs, took off my jacket, and turned back the sleeves of my shirt. April had descended on the city like a plague of hope: a clean smell of ozone in the mornings, the tuneless twittering of repatriated birds, bums coming out from the shelters to fill the benches and hollows of the park. The afternoon light was brilliant; traffic flowed smoothly uptown and I followed it, whistling a pop song from long ago. I had lost my virginity on a spring day not so different twenty-odd years before, and the up-thrusting jumble of Midtown skyscrapers seemed for a moment to recall the romantic glory of my teenage achievement. All over Manhattan, I knew, the doe-eyed farm girls who'd come to sing on Broadway were forgetting about last night's audition; they were putting on their roller skates and day-glow hot pants and heading for the park, where the broken-hearted immigrants could watch them in the lull between ten-hour shifts, thinking: ah, America.

It was so nice on the Avenue that I was almost sorry to reach the bar, but what can you do. The place was dark inside, one of a thousand identical cedar-paneled booze caves that dot the eastern half of the island between Grand Central and Ninety-Sixth. They would all be nearly empty at two in the afternoon. This was the secret of their two-o'clock appeal. I took a stool at the near end of the bar, placed an order, watched the barkeep set about polishing his glasses and taps and twist-handled spoons. Cabs sailed past the front window, pedestrians of every shape and size, dogs from the smaller breeds pissing in the tree stands. The sun cast a glow upon it all. Delusion is the sole refuge from chaos. I placed another order. I talked with the barman about the weather, the pace of his business, the condition of the Yankee pitching staff. Dust motes drifted through slanting shafts of light from the window. After a few refills I said, "Well, my brother's wife went off the deep end yesterday," though I hadn't intended to bring it up at all. I didn't even want to think about it. But I told the story front to back. I even made some new parts up.

When it was over the bartender just shook his head. His face remained impassive, true to the ancient neutrality of his trade. "That's a terrible story," he said.

"Terrible," I agreed.

"You got that right," said a man down the bar. He was the only other customer within earshot: bald, messy, veins on the nose. I couldn't tell his age, but whatever the number, he looked as if he'd earned it. "God help us, it's a hell of a world. Chinchillas. You know, a similar thing happened to a cousin of mine some years back..."

It was later than I had intended by the time I finally caught the train, but such things happen. To me they'd been happening more and more. I dropped into a seat that faced the wrong direction and floated back-first up through Harlem and the Bronx. I usually avoid those seats; tonight it seemed about right. I was drunk enough to feel a gentle spark of whimsical genius—gin, after all, lies at the heart of imagination—and as I watched the city recede into the night, I got to thinking about the resemblance between life and a wrong-way train seat, both of which move us forward as we look exclusively back. This seemed at the time like an insight of power and depth. Then I started thinking about what would happen if it worked the other way, and our view consisted entirely of what lies up the track. This perspective would explode the stubborn fantasy of optimism, but also excise memory—a mixed blessing, but not without compelling advantages. Of course the real disaster would be a world in which both past and future were visible all at once, and the entire scope of our debacle could be appreciated in sum at any given moment. So really, I decided, things could be a lot worse, and the broken street scenes of the Bronx gave way to the forests of Van Courtlandt Park, where deer can still be found, and then the leafy byways of exurbia, the jungle-gym backyards and basketball driveways, and the steady click-clack of the train car expressed a rhythm of constancy and progress as we glided northward through the country of my people and time.

Presently I fell asleep.

In my dream I was drinking in a hotel bar, alone in that loneliest of settings. It was someplace Mediterranean, the smell of rich expatriates and Pernod, but in the wrong season and deserted, the waiters standing in the corner, smoking cigarettes and discussing the next football season without much interest. Two women ate oysters with their backs to me at a front table and one of them said, "It was late March, I was walking down a hill to catch the Staten Island Ferry. It was snowing and I had chosen to walk because I loved the snow. Still do. I slipped on the ice and got run over by a bread truck. The funny part is that I wouldn't tell the police my name or age—I thought I might be in some kind of trouble, or maybe I was just delirious. A little of both, I suppose. I met him in the hospital, he was in the next bed. His own dog had just attacked him. Twenty-eight stitches in his cheek and arm, but he wasn't upset with the dog at all. I thought that was so touching. He was a jazz musician and we went to the clubs every night whether he was playing or not. I would sit at the bar with a Bloody Mary and a beer chaser, legs crossed, cigarette in a holder. I was a degenerate, and of course he screwed everybody. Divorce was the best thing that ever happened to me. Now my friends say I'm no fun to go out with, but..." I woke up thirsty and with a start to find that I hadn't been sleeping at all, or not exactly; the two women were seated across the aisle without their oysters. "You have to grow up sooner or later," concluded the storyteller. She was large and maybe fifty, in a floral print dress, something like a muumuu. Her companion was no more than fourteen. The entire scene threw me, and I wondered if it wasn't still a dream and about to shift again, to my childhood, to a Mexican prison, some other venue of fantasy. It did not. The train pulled into the station of my sleepy suburban town and I drove directly home, stopping only at the doughnut shop.

By the time I swung the car into our driveway and hoisted myself out, my wife was standing on the landing with a frown. "You're awfully late," she said.

"Nonsense," I said. "Kerwood never does anything awfully."

"Look what I found in Samantha's room." She held up a bag of cookies like a prosecutor presenting the defendant's bloody shawl.

"Cookies?"

"Oatmeal-raisin cookies."

I gasped. "Next she'll be smoking crank from an empty soda can."

"Christ, Steven. Can you be serious for ten seconds?" She dropped her eyes briefly and they softened into a plaintive expression. "It's just so *unhealthy.*"

"She's six."

"She's twelve pounds overweight."

"It's just baby fat."

"That's not what Dr. Ashburn thinks."

"Dr. Ashburn hates children," I informed her. "He became a pediatrician in order to torture them."

My wife sighed. "Dr. Ashburn does not hate children," she said slowly, measuring the words as if I myself were a child. "He just hates to see one becoming unhealthy. He says that Samantha needs to eat more protein and less fat, and now today I find these"—she shook the cookies—"in her sock drawer. Her goddamn sock drawer." Now she shook her head. "It's just so deceitful on top of everything else." The pain in her face was genuine and I leaned in to give her a kiss, to ask how work had been, to *soothe*, but the evening breeze must have brought her the gentle hint of a distillery. "Oh Christ," she said, pulling away. "You motherfucker."

I smiled: sheepish but still charming. "Relax. It was just a few with the boys after work."

"Damn it," she shouted, and then again, but louder, turning her back on me to go back in the house. "It's no fucking wonder, with the example you set," the back told me as it moved off down the front hall. "I'm the only adult in this family, for Christ's sake, and I have to..." The rest of the sentence disappeared around a corner and left me standing alone on the darkened vestibule.

(But don't be fooled: my wife is a woman of rare grace and charm, and if the pressures of life have put a crimp in her good humor, let it be known that my sympathies run deep. The pressures of course are severe. We all do the best we can. Charlotte and I, bound by the complexities of our history, were doing the best we could. Both of us were fresh out of college when we met at a rooftop party in Brooklyn Heights on the Fourth of July, and the fireworks were immediate. Long summer sky over the East River, charcoal smoke in her hair, a faint tang of salt on the skin—I think it would be fair to say that I've been hopelessly in love with her ever since, but it should also be pointed out that this phrase is open to several interpretations. Things had not been entirely well between us for some time. The process of growing apart from one's wife is both terribly unique and horrifically not unique, but I would suspect that it's a waste of strength in almost every case to pursue the thorny question of fault.)

I sighed, feeling the weight of my body in sudden disproportion, and attempted to gather myself. Elliot, the family dachshund (also portly), stood in the open doorway with his small head cocked to one side in a look that might well have been compassion. I gave him a doughnut.

It occurred to me that my stride was something less than steady as I moved along the hall, and I was relieved to make the dining room table without any embarrassing incidents. My wife and daughter were already eating. Samantha smiled at me;

Charlotte did not. I looked down at my plate and a nebulous glob of spinach lasagna looked back—leftovers from the weekend that had been left over for perfectly sensible reasons, but I shrewdly discerned that the moment for complaint was not at hand. And besides, there was Samantha's luminous gap-tooth smile to consider. She put her fork down and waved at me from across the table.

"Hi Daddy."

"Hi Sammy." I ventured a small wave of my own. "How was your day?"

"Well," she began, a little tentatively, shooting a sidelong glance at her mother, "school was good. Ms. Kendrick did a lesson about *astronauts*, and how on the moon you can jump up higher than buildings"—here she raised her chubby right arm to its fullest extension, palm down, to indicate the height of buildings—"and then we did a spelling lesson and learned all the vegetables and then we did cursive and I got a prize for writing my name prettiest."

"Wow," I said, genuinely impressed. "What was the prize?"

"I got to be first in line for recess." She held up her left index finger, a delicate little sausage link, to illustrate firstness.

"Super."

"Yeah, but at recess me and Lucinda Bartholomew caught two sixth graders kissing behind the equipment shed and it was gross."

"Ewww." I soured my face to demonstrate confederate disgust. "Were they using their tongues?"

"Gross!" Sam squealed. "People don't *do* that."

"Some people do."

"Nu-uh."

I leaned over the table and narrowed my eyes. "They do," I said, "for reals."

"Gross!" she squealed again, and the squeal dissolved into a lilting giggle that seemed, in my simple, mildly impaired mind, to animate the room.

"Samantha," said my wife, "you haven't eaten much of your lasagna."

"But I'm not hungry."

Charlotte sighed and dabbed the corners of her mouth with a napkin. "You still have to eat your lasagna, honey, because it's what we're having for dinner."

"*But I'm not hungry.*"

"The only reason you're not hungry is because you ate too many cookies after school. Now eat your lasagna. It's good for you."

Sam gazed down at her plate and began absently plowing the pasta with her fork. Charlotte shot me a dark look that represented my cue to say something appropriately stern and parental. "Your mother's right," I told Sam. "Lasagna is very good for you. There's a lot of protein in the soy cheese."

She continued the non-committal plowing. "I went over to Lucinda Bartholomew's house for dinner and they had lasagna with regular cheese and it tasted better."

"Yes," I explained, "but Lucinda will become obese and end up taking her brother to the prom."

"What's a prom?"

Charlotte produced an exasperated groan and stood up

from the table."God almighty, Steven." She winced. "I'm going to take a bath. Samantha, you need to finish your lasagna. Is that clear?"

Sam nodded, although the directive was intended for me. My wife left the room and Samantha and I listened to her feet tramp up the stairs. I smiled weakly at my daughter. "So she found the cookies, huh?"

Sam looked down at her lap. "Yeah. And she was *mad.*"

"It's OK, kiddo." I reached across and squeezed the plumpness of her tiny hand. "We've just got to hide them better, that's all."

"I put them in the sock drawer. She's getting more snoopy."

"Yes, I can see that." We frowned at each other. "But look what I got." I produced the bag of doughnuts from under the table.

Sam's pudgy face immediately lit up again, and I placed the bag in front of her, scraping her plate onto mine and setting it aside. "What kind?" she asked.

"One glazed, and one Boston cream."

"Boston cream! Boston cream!" She clapped her hands the way children clap their hands, without angling them to avoid the collision of fingers.

"Dig in," I said, and in she dug. There are of course the French masters, impressionists, expressionists, whateverists, with their paintings of lily pads and naked women—I'll trade them anytime for the chance to watch a child eat a Boston cream doughnut. A splotchy layer of custard rapidly engulfed Samantha's mouth, her cheeks, her chin and hands and wrists. She mauled the pastry like a polar bear devouring a wounded harp seal, and I was compelled to let her have the glazed as well for an encore.

"Well, slugger," I said when she had finished, and sat beaming at me from amid the carnage, "what do you feel like doing tonight?"

"I want to watch TV."

My mouth fell open. "That's amazing," I replied, "because *I* want to watch TV too."

"Yay!" she said.

"Yay!" I said.

So we watched TV. It was inspiring, filled, as always, with happiness and resolution: the injured doe recovers, the family escapes from the meat freezer, even engine grease is no match for the miraculous detergent. It all seemed so contrary to the unfolding of my day, yet lulled my daughter into an easy sleep beside me just the same. Carrying her rotund little sleep heavy and twelve pounds overweight body up the stairs, I felt some faint glimmer of heroism myself. It was a fragile sensation that hung on just long enough for me to tuck her into bed and hit the light.

Returning to the kitchen, I found Charlotte balancing our checkbook at the table. She was chewing on her lower lip, as has always been her habit in moments of concentration, and I was able to stand in the doorframe and watch her for a few delicate seconds before my presence attracted her glance.

"Is she in bed?"

"She is."

"She needs new soccer cleats," my wife said, tapping the

checkbook with the butt of her pen, "and the piano teacher is raising her rates again. My car needs new tires and the house has to be painted. And my mother wants me to come out to Scottsdale again before summer."

"We have plenty of money," I reminded her.

"Yes," she said. There was a pause. "I just have this feeling," she said, "that we're not going to be able to do it."

"You can fly out of Newark. It won't cost much."

"That's not what I mean. You know what I mean."

I furrowed my brow as if in thought, and, sitting down, looked into her eyes with a directness that was intended to convey the impression of honesty. "Yes," I said, "yes, I know. But listen: everything's going to be fine."

Charlotte looked down at the table and began massaging her temple. "It's not that I'm mad at you. I mean, I am mad at you, but that's not the point. You just seem to be going through something that I can't help you with. I'm not sure I have the capacity for it, and even if I did, it feels like..." She trailed off with a vacant hand gesture and the sentence came apart in the air.

I smiled. "Things will get better. They always do."

My wife weighed that brilliant supposition quietly, or pretended to weigh it, and gave me a vague nod. "I'm going to bed," she said.

"Right," I said, "well, I might futz around down here for a little while, but I'll be up before too long."

She came around the table and paused, standing in front of me as if to add some further comment, and I watched ominous clouds of tenderness and resignation drift across her face. She reached out to smooth my hair and brush away the loose strands that clung to my forehead. "That's fine," she said, "that's fine, take your time," and then she walked out of the room.

I sat there at the table, listening to the clock ticking above the sink and the sink dripping below the clock. Elliot waddled in like a kielbasa on matchsticks, wagging his tail for no good reason. I went to the high cabinet for the club soda bottle that did not contain club soda and retreated with it to the backyard, accompanied by a glass of ice and the oddly constructed dog.

The day had been difficult, but the lawn's soft grass beneath my feet and the early spring nighttime all around me provided the hope of a benevolent conclusion. Sitting at our picnic table, which seemed to hold the promise of warmer weather in the very smell of its rotting wood, I poured myself a drink. The crickets chirped, a bird warbled unseen from a high branch. Elliot relieved himself near my foot. I threw his chew toy not very far, and he went to get it not very quickly. A car passed on the street, and somewhere a sprinkler came to life. Elliot barked casually at a squirrel. The crickets chirped, a bird warbled unseen from a high branch. I poured myself another drink.

Midway through drink three my attention was called to the Gundersons' bedroom window, which they had neglected to shut against the mildness of the evening. The soft but unmistakable sounds of conjugal affection issued from inside. This development struck me not with the guilty tingle of voyeurism, but rather with a gentler warmth, an acknowledgment of something tender and universal. The divinity of love, the softness of spring evenings: these things touch us all. For a moment the weight of the past dropped away; it was nothing like the night I myself had shared with Nancy Gunderson. That had been several months before in the hostility of a cold November darkness. Charlotte was traveling on business, although truthfully I don't know whether or not Nancy was aware of this when she called my house after eleven o'clock on a Monday to ask if I might take a look at her broken television set.

I am embarrassed to admit that this was not the only dalliance in which I have indulged since my marriage. Each has left me with a similar hollowness, an exponential magnification of the withdrawal and sense of loss that always follows the crucial moment of passion. Each has burdened me likewise with a handful of unpleasant recollections that seem to be the only surviving details. In Nancy's case, these include the collection of ceramic Easter bunnies on her dresser, the dark hairs on her upper lip that become visible at close range, and the way she asked about Samantha as I was hastily putting on my shoes. But who among us is above reproach? I once returned from a Sunday golf outing to find a monogrammed cigarette lighter in the downstairs bathroom. Samantha had conveniently been sent to stay with my parents for the weekend and my wife does not smoke. I chose not to press Charlotte about it, but for the rest of my days on this earth a grim shadow of suspicion will darken my face whenever I am introduced to a man with the initials H.C.; there is a patient here at Dr. _____'s named Howard Chase, and we are not friendly.

Fireworks. For years Charlotte and I remained giddily in awe of one another, stunned by the generosity of life, astonished by the transcendent possibilities of the human body, etc. Then one day I realized that we were no longer any of these things, and it was impossible to recall whether the change had been sudden or not sudden. Charlotte must have felt the same, but neither one of us wanted to come right out and say anything. We decided to have a child instead. It was, in a way, easier than discussing our relationship, and the early returns were excellent. With Samantha around, there was always Samantha to talk about. Her bodily functions alone could provide enough fodder to stave off awkward silence for weeks at a stretch. But in time I think we discovered that raising a daughter only throws certain grievances into starker relief; it does not solve the core problems. Not that I even remember what the core problems were, not that I ever understood them. Boredom, fatigue, lack of imagination, failure to change at the same rate or in all the same ways—drop them in a hat and take your pick. The story is hardly unusual. It may be the least unusual story in the world, but its harrowing mundanity only deepens the mystery for me. You can hand your savings over to a head shrinker, you can make a list of reasons longer than your arm. The very idea of reasons implies that we are living in a world of comprehensible phenomena, but the evidence argues otherwise. Whales beach themselves, lemmings follow one another over cliffs, a father murders his son over a game of cards: these things happen every day.

Up in their bedroom the Gundersons continued to frolic. But then again, I thought, who can say if it's really the Gundersons at all? Who can say if the affection is conjugal or even affectionate? It could just as easily be Nancy and the television repairman; Nancy and the gardener; Nancy and the pool boy; Nancy and Pastor McDonald; Nancy and a wandering minstrel from the White Plains Renaissance Fair. It could just as easily be Tom Gunderson and a young French sailor named Jean Luc, who makes careful note of where the wealthy American's pants have been discarded, the fat wallet bulging in the back left pocket. The truth is that you never know. It's frightening, really. I took up the empty bottle and empty glass and went inside, listing like a dinghy in a storm; the kitchen and the dining room pitched disturbingly, port to starboard, starboard to port. I paused in the hallway to steady myself. I climbed the stairs with care, entered my room, and sat down on edge of the bed. "Charlotte," I said, or tried to say. The name came out a little thickly. I was shaking my wife gently, or trying to shake her gently. "The strangest thing just happened. Listen. I was in the backyard—"

"Stop," said a voice that had not been sleeping.

"Over at the—"

"Stop. Steven, please stop."

"OK," I said. "But I heard them."

My wife said, "You have to go. I can't do this tonight."

I nodded my head slowly in the dark. "It was strange, that's all. A lot of things."

"Steven."

I turned on the lamp, knocking a few items off the night-stand along the way. She propped herself up on both elbows and looked at me. Her eyes were red and puffy, but not like from sleep. She sniffled. "The Gundersons," I said.

"Please Steven, just go."

"I wanted to tell you something."

"Please," she said, "I can't do this tonight."

I cleared my throat. "Would you like me to go?"

"Yes."

I furrowed my brow and thought, or tried to think. It was a difficult moment. I said, "Ben called today. Rebecca has gone off the deep end."

Now Charlotte nodded. She sniffled again and wiped her nose with the back of her hand. She repeated the word "go" very softly.

So I went. Closing the door lightly on my way out, I was left in the hallway and some confusion. The house was silent, and it was one of those silences that may paradoxically be referred to as deafening. Elliot was giving me that half-cocked look again, only this time I didn't like it; I didn't give him a doughnut. I picked him up and headed for the laundry room.

Tucked into the crook of my arm like a football, he betrayed no resentment or fear. Death comes for us all eventually: the icy hand, the reaper's scythe. When it comes for me, I can only hope to meet it with the same grace and courage displayed by my corpulent dachshund as we made our way downstairs. Elliot maintained the faultless sympathy of his expression, as all great martyrs do, a fact I have since reflected on considerably and now find to be quite moving. At the time I was not moved. I opened the dryer and we stood there, the two of us, like a Polynesian king and a virgin on the rim of a volcano.

Then a funny thing happened, funny like milk left out on the counter overnight: my daughter appeared in the open doorway, barefoot in azure blue pajamas, her curly brown hair pressed flat on one side. The pajamas were covered with little red rocket ships traveling cheerfully to small yellow stars, but

Sam's face was darkened by a look that bespoke preternatural comprehension of the circumstances. "Daddy," she asked, "what are you doing?"

How is one to respond in such a situation—what is the *right* thing? We are confronted, at any given point in life, with an infinity of potential choices, a maze, a yawning chasm of options, and it has always seemed to me that some law of justice or evolution should grant us a commensurate ability to make our decisions wisely. Looking back on that unfortunate impasse in the laundry room, I am again reminded that such is not the case. It was one of those moments when time itself seems to hang on the outcome of human drama: the priceless vase slips off the mantle, the grenade rolls into the foxhole, the oblivious child steps out from a line of parked cars. I looked from Samantha, to Elliot, to the dryer's gaping crater, to my own phantom reflection in the windowpane. They all looked back expectantly, as if the explanation for human frailty might walk out of my mouth and hold a press conference on the washing machine.

"Daddy?" Samantha asked again. "What are you doing?"

What am I doing? I'm getting better, that's what. Bee ee tee, tee ee are. All the doctors assure me of this, although they assure me in the next breath that the road is long, that it's harmful to impose a timeline on the process, and perfectly normal for the Valium to cause this charming urinary retention. They are men of science, of course, men of reason and strict methodologies; they maintain that the broken lives entrusted to their care are merely cases of chemical imbalance and genetic predilection, problems with causes, problems with solutions. But I wonder how the world truly looks through their eyes. We are broken — myself, Walter Hogan, Howard Chase, all the rest — but when they leave here at night, our doctors, does the world outside seem to them as if it's not? Do they sit on the porch each evening, sipping lemonade and watching the sun go down, or do they beat their wives, abuse their prescription books, and dress in women's underwear?

I am getting better, but nobody ever says exactly what "better" means, and I don't ask. Not asking questions seems to be part of what getting better entails. I am told that through sobriety, in time, I will come to see things more clearly, but this strikes me as a misapprehension of the problem. Or a refusal to admit that the fundamental problem exists. My brother comes to see me when he can, and he seems to have aged ten years in these last two months. We don't talk about it exactly, but I can tell that he understands some part of what I understand. Rebecca is not getting better. She gives no indication of knowing Ben when he visits, and has become convinced that a certain small stuffed koala bear is actually her child. She sings it lullabies, allows it to feed at her breast, and, on several occasions, has attempted to drown it in the toilet water. "But the thing of it," Ben tells me, "the thing of it is her eyes. You look into them and Rebecca isn't there. I know my wife, and she isn't there anymore. There's just this darkness..." And of course, he says, the doctors can't explain this phenomenon at all.

FAUNTLEROY'S
GHOST

Stucky was not a screenwriter by trade, but the market for historical fiction was poor and it seemed incredible that no one had ever made a bio pic about Trotsky. Trotsky was the perfect Hollywood subject. History had conspired to preserve his innocence. Not uniformly, of course—he had commanded the Red Army in the Civil War, and declined to flinch from the harsh realities of command. Whole villages loyal to the Whites were slaughtered. Pregnant mothers hacked to bits, children set afire. As a Utopian theoretician, it must have been terrible for him. One imagines Trotsky on a visit to the front, alone in the small hours in a field tent on the steppe east of Saratov: October, snow on the ground, a bitter wind bringing word of winter from Siberia. Trotsky sips a vodka and allows himself a rare moment to reflect. For the most part one must press relentlessly ahead, but now the camp is quiet and his generals are all asleep. Sleep comes easily for them; the burden rests with Trotsky. Yesterday he rode past two soldiers raping a corpse in a ditch by the road. The world cannot be remade in a tidy fashion. None of this was in Stucky's script. In Stucky's script it was Trotsky alone who had not been fooled by Stalin, who had stood up to the tyrant when everyone else was forsaking the Revolution to save their own skins. It was Trotsky alone who rose to give truth a voice as his comrades wilted on all sides. He did so caring nothing for his own life, which would first be made wretched and then end at last in violence. He must have known in advance how the whole thing would play out. This was the stuff of Hollywood: Hollywood loves a martyr.

Stucky hadn't been to Los Angeles for years when his agent called to announce that he'd arranged a couple pitch meetings for the script. "I had to call in some markers," he said, "this idea's a dud."

"Mmm," said Stucky.

"Don't get me wrong, bud, I love it, but nobody wants to make a commie flick. Proletarian revolt is like a punch line. Yesterday's papers. Individuals are all the rage, know what I mean?"

"Trotsky is an individual."

"He's a shill for the masses. Strictly passé."

"I see."

"Don't pout, Tiger. You're a genius to hear me tell it. All I'm saying is get your game face on—this baby isn't gonna sell herself."

"I will don my game face."

"'Don'—that's a great verb. Look, get a little sun while you're down there, Ace. Play some beach volleyball. Try to relax."

Yes, he would try to relax. February in Seattle was even worse than usual, endless days of drizzle and bone-damp fog, raccoon shit clogging the gutters on Stucky's roof and causing leaks to appear in the kitchen and dining room, but he found that he was not looking forward to his trip. Los Angeles seemed to represent something dystopic in Stucky's brain, a harrowing vision of the future, the victory of fragmentation and style. This was a common idea, an article of the conventional wisdom culled from Nathaniel West and a thousand films. Also, Stucky's last visit to L.A., nearly a decade ago, had been occasioned by a brief, volatile love affair—a "fling," to use the awful term—that ended in confusion and tears in the parking lot of an art deco carwash on Sunset Boulevard. Shouting after his lover as her Hyundai peeled out onto Sunset, watching her upraised middle finger stare back at him as it receded toward Los Feliz, standing in the sun in a blue suit he'd been wearing for three days, Stucky realized that he had unwittingly entered the dream logic of the great and sprawling city: he was enacting a scene from a movie. No, he did not want to go back to Los Angeles, but the screenplay represented his lone financial and professional hope. His last novel, *The Love Song of Charles de Gaulle*, had sold so poorly that he would have to work under an alias if he ever wished to publish in the United States again. He would fly down on a Tuesday and make his first pitch the next morning, with a second meeting to follow the day after. On Friday morning he would fly home. The schedule left him with plenty of downtime, and it was for this reason, perhaps against his better judgment, that he decided to call his old friend Bobby Raskin.

"Stucky, you old so-and-so!" Raskin said on the phone. "How the hell are you? Still suffering for art?"

"Terribly. My pain is heroic. How's the ruthless world of high finance?"

"Ruthless? Who told you ruthless? These pussycats just want to purr, my friend. Give 'em the milk and they lick it right up, if you catch my drift."

"Sure. They love the milk."

"I got some fossil Jews at my club who used to spar with Meyer Lansky for the top shelf trim down in old Havana. I watch them light cigars on the terrace—beautiful Cohibas, they never run out. That's as close as Raskin gets to ruthless these days."

"I'm glad to hear that," Stucky said. He hadn't spoken to Raskin in a long time, but Raskin had not changed. Raskin never changed. This, in fact, was the purpose of Raskin. Whenever you stepped in gum or were shat on by a bird, you could take comfort in the knowledge that somewhere in the world, at that very moment, Raskin was probably getting blown in a limo. Life was chaos, Stucky felt, but even chaos had its limits. Its limits were Raskin. He explained that his game was venture capital now—running a "boutique" firm that "dabbled in a little of everything." Hustling, in other words, turning profit wherever he found it, above board and below, making money as other men breathed. Venture capital was new vocabulary; for Raskin, the game itself was timeless. He and Stucky agreed to meet for lunch, and then perhaps head out to Santa Anita for the races.

"I got a colt going off in the fourth. Magnificent animal, you have to see him — a twenty-to-one shot. Jesus, it's like free money."

It was all free to Raskin. "I'll bring my piggy bank," Stucky said, watching the water drip from his ceiling into a Crockpot he'd set on the kitchen floor. He had no doubt that Raskin's horse would win — unless he, Stucky, should venture to place a bet on it, in which case the "magnificent animal" would probably spontaneously combust.

His flight left Sea-Tac in the early gloom of a winter afternoon, two hours late. They were barely off the ground when it became clear that someone aboard had terrible gas. The rank smell bloomed in untraceable waves; everyone sought to exonerate themselves with looks of suitable disgust. Stucky had no choice but to join them. The failure to glance suspiciously around was like an admission of guilt. A complex dance of smell and mien: no one said a word aloud. At LAX the smoking pens were full of Asian men. Stucky drifted past, down the gleaming concourse, as the gentle lilt of a woman's voice called strangers to the courtesy phone. He arrived late at the hotel and watched a movie on cable. The movie was about a golden retriever who learns to play piano. The dog's owner works at a ramshackle beach club, but developers want to buy the club and turn it into a high-end resort. The landlord is prepared to sell—the club will close unless its employees can somehow raise enough money to match the developers' offer. The situation seems hopeless until Jenny discovers the dog's fantastic talent. At first no one believes her. Later, a concert is organized. Stucky fell asleep and dreamed of Trotsky playing "Great Balls of Fire" in Moscow at the Party Congress of 1926.

In the morning he pitched his script. The meeting was held in a windowless conference room in Century City. A middle-aged studio apparatchik by the name of Bunsen—"like the burner"—greeted Stucky warmly. He made small talk for a few minutes and then asked for the pitch. Latte foam clung to his upper lip. The walls of the room were bare. Stucky nodded, drew a breath.

"The great question of modernity," he began, "is whether the forces of which history is comprised have grown so large that their outcomes may be considered, insofar as the individual is concerned, inevitable, or whether these great forces instead remain vulnerable to the influence of a single man's life. In other words: Are we necessarily the victims of history, or may history, in effect, become our victim? Trotsky stands at the very center of this question by seeming to evince both notions at once..."

He walked Bunsen through Trotsky's political origins, his crucial years with Lenin in London, their period of estrangement, the Revolution, the shock of a victory that shook the world, the Civil War, and then Stalin's slow consolidation of power— the force of Stalin's narrow genius, his mind burned clean of every goal but one. First he joins Kamenev and Zinoviev in the troika; the other two criticize Trotsky, but Stalin hangs back. He greets Trotsky fondly at Politburo meetings while Kamenev and Zinoviev look away. He plays the middle, quietly stacking the bureaucracy with henchmen. Trotsky sees his allies ousted one by one, he alone sees Stalin's game—but direct confrontation will split the Party and threaten the young nation for which Trotsky has given so much. His faith is with the Party; the Party is the people's will; truth will out if the Party endures. But Stalin gradually compounds Trotsky's isolation, moving with the force of a glacier, wiping the landscape clean. Kamenev and Zinoviev see their true foe too late. They bow to Stalin but Trotsky will not; Trotsky chooses exile in Siberia and continues his opposition, corresponding tirelessly with whoever will listen, distributing eloquent critiques of the Comintern. "Socialism needs democracy," he writes, "like the human body needs oxygen." Stalin orders his final deportation in 1929.

February, the streets of Alma-Alta drifted deep with snow: Trotsky packs his family into a truck for their arduous journey to the railhead at Frunze, 250 kilometers across the soaring Tian Shan range on snowbound Kazakh roads. A train will carry them west from there, toward Constantinople and the mercies of a nameless fate. But Trotsky hardly feels he is beaten. He watches the majestic, forbidding terrain unfold, this Soviet Union born largely of his single will. He's been forced out before—twice by the Czar, and twice on the wings of rebellion he's returned. The story of his life is the story of history and struggle is its one true name. Trotsky burns with purpose, with fidelity to his view of time and the destiny of men. Already they have killed his daughter; he will live to see his other children murdered too; he will live to see the Moscow show trials: Zinoviev admitting everything, admitting whatever they want — then Kamenev, then others. The scope of the tragedy will be difficult to grasp. Trotsky dreamed of remaking the world and then remade it, only to discover he had created a monster. Poignant historical irony. Now he is passing a lake. Trotsky sips vodka from a pewter flask and through the window of the bouncing truck observes the lake. Framed by jutting peaks, its surface is a sheet of ice blown clean in places by the wind. Dusk. Night is coming but has yet to arrive. Trotsky thinks: they will stop at nothing; they will murder my children; they will murder everyone; the sunset is brilliant where it strikes the ice; the fish are sleeping yonder in a brilliant cage of light. He repeats this last phrase silently over and over. The camera zooms in as his lips mouth the words. It became clear about halfway through that Bunsen had ceased to listen.

He nodded when Stucky was done. "I love the Russians," Bunsen said. "The Russians are a magnificent people."

"Yes," said Stucky. "Magnificent."

"Billionaires growing like weeds over there in Moscow."

"Oligarchs and gangsters. Many success stories."

"There you go." Bunsen chuckled. "I laid this Russian girl in New York last year, the daughter of some gas tycoon. You wouldn't believe the kind of money she had. We met at a premier someplace downtown, both of us totally blotto. I'd have to be drunk to lay a girl that fat — she must have been pushing three bills. But she had a driver waiting and a suite at the W on Union Square, so I said what the hell, let's go whaling. We screwed like no tomorrow, man, it was gross. I almost barfed in the morning just thinking about it. Then I laid her again. Worst thing ever. Then I'm getting dressed and she's like, Oh, my little babushka, let my driver take you home. Sure, I say, why not. Treat me right, you horny orca. I go downstairs and there's her driver with the car. Man, I must've smelled like open ass, and I didn't feel too good either. Screw a girl that big and you feel it in your joints, am I right? So I get in the backseat and tell the guy where to go, and then I look down and what do you think I see? It's her cell phone. She left her phone in the car the night before, like the damn thing must have fallen out of her clutch bag while we were dry humping or something. So you know what I did?"

Stucky shook his head. He had no idea.

"I threw it out the window." Bunsen stood and offered his hand. "The script sounds great. We'll call your guy."

Stucky boarded his rental car and floated up Santa Monica Boulevard, thinking Santa Monica Boulevard thoughts—the desolation of modernity, history's inexorable thrust toward aesthetic ruin, the magnetism of anonymous bars at the lunch hour. A neon cocktail glass, with its neon olive and neon stir, is a symbol that speaks the Esperanto of despair, to mix a metaphor as some friendly barkeep might mix a cold Old Fashioned on the rocks. The traffic was heavy. Beautiful women, alone in their vehicles, alone behind designer shades, prattled into cell phones as they drove. Elsewhere in the city, alone in other vehicles, accessorized with other designer gear, square-jawed men were prattling back, landscaped body hair lurking beneath their clothes. Los Angeles like a tawdry fantasy of late capitalism, etc. Stucky had come here to hawk the tale of a Marxist prophet. Maybe his agent was right. He turned off Santa Monica and drifted through the sun-dappled streets of Brentwood toward the address he'd scrawled on a Post-It note in his kitchen two days before. Lunch with Raskin was unlikely to make him feel better. One did not seek Raskin out in order to feel better. Sometimes it was unclear to Stucky why they had remained friends for so long. He arrived at the house ten minutes early to discover that it was on fire.

Fire engines and police cars blocked the street. Stucky pulled his rental to the curb and stepped out. A beautiful day. The marine layer had burned off, giving way to a crystalline blue sky. The air was thin and weightless, stirred by a light breeze from the water. Dense black smoke poured from what was left of Raskin's home. The smoke rose in thick plumes pulled slowly apart on the breeze. One half of the house was charred down to the frame, orange flames still licking the crossbeams as firemen stood in the yard, patiently wielding their hoses. Their bearing had a post-urgent flavor, like baseball players in the ninth inning of a blowout. Stucky made his way through a small crowd of spectators to the caution tape, where two cops were standing guard.

"This is my brother's house," Stucky told them. "I was supposed to meet him here for lunch."

"Name?"

"Raskin."

The cops looked at each other. Then they looked at Stucky. One of them lifted the tape.

They crossed to the driveway, where a woman stared at the smoking house and wept. She was blond, small, elegantly sobbing. Uniformed men milled around her, but no one wanted to get too close. A plainclothes cop faced her at a safe remove, pen and pad in hand, but he wasn't asking any questions. Into this mix Stucky was introduced, ominously, as "the brother."

"You imbeciles," the woman growled, "Bobby doesn't even have a brother." She paused to gather a sob. "I mean *didn't* even."

The men all turned to Stucky.

"Didn't?" Stucky said. "What do you mean, *didn't*?"

A foolish question. Nobody answered.

"My name is Stucky," Stucky said. "I'm an old friend of Raskin's." He looked down at his feet.

When he looked back up the woman had taken a half step toward him, as if to get a better view. She scrutinized Stucky with eyes the color of a swimming pool. Her mouth turned slightly upward at the corners, like the Joker. Hair tangled, face flushed, she bore all the marks of passion; she was stunning, Stucky realized. *Raskin*, he thought, *you son of a bitch*. Such a woman would never weep for Stucky.

"Ben Stucky?" she said. "From Seattle?"

They sat that evening on adjacent stools in one of the nameless taprooms Stucky had admired along Santa Monica. Nathalie— her name was Nathalie—seemed dazed. The police had kept her all afternoon; they were treating Raskin's death as a homicide. She sipped a glossy Cosmo from a martini glass. "Whatever you do feels wrong," she said. "Christ, look at me — my boyfriend was blown up today and now I'm getting blitzed in a dive bar to Mötley Crüe."

Indeed, "Don't Go Away Mad (Just Go Away)" spilled from the jukebox at moderate volume. The sun's parting rays slanted through two dingy portholes over the bar, falling to the floor in slabs of moted dust. Was she getting blitzed? Stucky nursed his second whiskey. Already his head had begun to rise pleasantly away from his shoulders. He turned to enjoy Nathalie's profile as she stared absently at the many-colored bottles in their tripartite hierarchy along the wall. Booze like Gaul thrice divided. Various expressions played across her clever mouth: a complex discourse of confusion, anger, grief — it was hard to tell. She sighed and looked down.

"This bar has a carpet. There should never be carpet in a bar. You should never go to a carpeted bar after your boyfriend gets blown up."

But where then? Raskin was dead; this shabby cantina was the keening of their souls. Stucky leaned back to drain his glass. The ice slid down and struck his teeth with a satisfying *click*.

"In India," he offered, motioning to the bartender for a refill, "Hindu wives were once expected to hurl themselves onto their husbands' burning funereal biers."

"Cute — but I got there too late. The cops and firemen were already on the scene. I don't think they would have let me do it."

Stucky nodded. "In Nazi Germany, on the other hand, Goebbels banned mourning of the war dead entirely. It was officially regarded as an honor to give one's life in defense of the Reich. Sadness thus became unpatriotic."

"Interesting. Keep going."

The barman delivered Stucky's new drink and drifted away—a gorgeous barman, with sculpted features and the biceps of a stevedore. The jukebox moved on to "Kickstart My Heart."

"OK. In certain Inuit cultures the dead are unable to pass into the next world until a loved one slays a narwhal and grinds its horn into fine powder, which is then added to a poultice of seal fat with which the naked corpse is rubbed to release the soul."

"I like that one."

"Good." He sampled the whiskey. Delicious. "I made it up."

She laughed and flashed a sly smile, sidelong, without showing any teeth. "I see why Bobby liked you," she said, lifting her glass. "This shit tastes like Robitussin. Why don't you buy me a nip of whatever you're having, Ben Stucky from Seattle."

He bought her a nip of what he was having.

"Here's to never getting old. I don't think it would've suited Bobby anyway."

"No," Stucky agreed. "We should all have Raskin's luck."

Their glasses touched.

"Boom," Nathalie whispered.

The bomb had gone off in Raskin's study around eleven o'clock. He was apparently alone in the house—Nathalie was on her way over from the airport, to which she had just returned after spending four days with her parents in St. Louis. Raskin called from his landline no more than five minutes before the blast. He asked her to pick up some olives and a fifth of Tanqueray.

Now she said, "Tell me a story, Ben. Just anything—anything about Bobby."

"Do you want it to be true?"

"That's up to you."

She turned to face him and canted her weight slightly forward, nibbling her lower lip. The turquoise of her eyes was borderline unnatural, like the pastel shades of a colorized film. Her top, though decorously black, featured a plunging neckline uncommon to mourning garb. The neckline's effect became more generous as she leaned in.

"OK," Stucky said. "One time me and Raskin went after the same girl. This was in college, and both of us liked this one girl."

"Lucky girl."

"Sure, she hit the jackpot. An embarrassment of riches for Deborah Anne Pagel. Debbie. She was mine first, of course, but what could that matter to Raskin? A detail. To Raskin it mattered not at all. I met her at a jazz club on Shattuck and we went on a couple dates, two or three dates, and it was going pretty well. What I mean is that I liked her, we had fun together, she was smart—tall, thin, wore her hair in braids. Came from Santa Barbara, a classy girl, writing her thesis on Flaubert. Maybe you're wondering if I'd 'sealed the deal.' Well, the answer is no—we hadn't, I hadn't—*yet*—but things were going well. Then she disappears. Breaks a date one weekend, won't return my calls the next week—abracadabra.

Am I hurt? Yes, I'm somewhat hurt. But these things happen, right? You never see it coming. Of course I'd made the mistake of introducing her to Raskin, but I didn't see the connection at first."

He paused and swirled the ice in his glass. Round and round went the ice, booze-wet, melting slow. Nathalie said nothing.

"Then one night I'm walking past Raskin's building. This is maybe ten days after Debbie goes poof. Raskin's got this Jimmy Smith record of mine that he borrowed and I kind of want it back, or maybe I just want to talk, maybe I'm just lonely or something. But anyway, I go on up to Raskin's place unannounced. You can probably see where I'm heading with this."

Nathalie pursed her lips, philosophically. "What were they doing?"

"Nothing. They were drinking, they were drunk. All their clothes on, listening to Handel or some bullshit."

"Maybe it was innocent."

"Raskin had a pubic hair in his teeth."

She choked on a laugh, turning away to hide her face. The jukebox fell quiet. The bartender looked up from his magazine. Outside, on Santa Monica, cars were moving east and west, whispering gently of the great metal tide. All these years later and Stucky could still see with perfect clarity the kinky black hair glistening from its perch in Raskin's grin.

"I'm sorry," Nathalie said, "I'm sorry, I shouldn't laugh — but I guess you forgave him eventually."

"Sure I did. Why not? Everyone forgives Raskin."

"No," she said, gathering herself. Stucky watched the water pool suddenly in her eyes. "Apparently not everyone."

The sky over Westwood was synthetically bright, clouds of noxious smog lit yellow like the center of a fresh bruise. Stucky returned late to his hotel, feeling strangely ecstatic, a lightness in his bones. In the lobby a pretty Latin girl stood near the elevators with a leashed ferret. She smiled at Stucky; the ferret did not. How mystifying and full of possibility the world seemed. True, Raskin was dead, his old pal Raskin, but to feel bad for Raskin was to misunderstand and perhaps dishonor him. This was a man who had smuggled contraband Aztec relics up from Oaxaca in the hold of an old racing sloop and once had sex on an airplane with Feiticeira, the Vanna White of Brazil. To die before his time in a mysterious explosion at a fashionable Brentwood address was a stroke of Raskin's peculiar genius, really. Stucky would die alone in the Lysoled quiet of some flowerless hospital room, plastic tubing up his urethra and nose. The day nurse comes in whistling a show tune, empties the bedpan before she even realizes—this was how Stucky would die.

But in the meantime: life. Back in his room he felt vital, too wound up for sleep. He drew back the curtain and stood gazing out on the city's long carpet of lights stretching away to the east, toward the mountains and the endless scrub brush desert and the great brutal sweep of America churning away in the dark. Nathalie was so hot. It wasn't even that Stucky wanted to lay her, exactly, but more that beauty of her kind bespoke a fabulous potential swirling gently in the ether. Certainly they had made a connection. In her hour of need, in her moment of desolation and loss, he had bought her strong drink and made her laugh. He was sympathetic but not mawkish—a difficult balance to strike. It was a hazard of his solitary existence that Stucky somtimes forgot how socially adroit he could be. At certain times, in short bursts, he could be very adroit, socially. He could make incisive remarks, he had an interesting mind—interestingly dark. Should call her tomorrow and check in, just to see how she's doing. Though he didn't have her number, she had his. There was noise in the closet. Stucky turned from the window. The closet door opened and Raskin stepped out.

They stood there looking at each other for a few long seconds. Raskin smiled. He spread his hands, palms displayed, and cocked one foot up on its heel in a vaudevillian gesture of *ta da.*

"Raskin," Stucky hissed. "I should have known."

"Of course you should have, buddy, but don't beat yourself up." He opened a gold Zippo and sparked the flame, brushing it across the tip of a cigarette that appeared between his lips. "Pleasant evening?"

"She's marvelous," Stucky blurted out. "She's astonishing."

"Sure she is. A real gem."

Raskin pulled a deep drag off his butt, drawing the flesh down tight across his cheekbones—giving him, however briefly, the skeletal cast of dead man. The truth was that he looked terrible. His weight was down and he seemed not to have shaved for days, or maybe to have shaved poorly. His whole face appeared boiled. His beige linen suit was dirty, the coat too short in the sleeves. He cradled a fat manila envelope under his left arm.

"What's going on, Raskin?"

"You don't seem very happy to see me."

"Naturally I'm thrilled. You look like shit."

"I feel worse than that," he said, tapping ash on the carpet. His rakish grin dropped away. He moved a little too quickly to scratch an itch behind his ear. "You have to help me, Stucky."

Stucky crossed his arms and considered his old chum. Raskin, who had it all and rarely with much effort, who had seen Nathalie naked and no doubt enticed her into acts of uncommon lewdness—somehow it was always Raskin who needed *your* help. Stucky nodded very slowly but did not speak.

"Please," Raskin said, "don't be that way, Stuck. It was dangerous for me to come here, even, but I didn't know where else to turn."

"Raskin never runs out of friends."

He waved his hand dismissively. "You'd be surprised. Pals dry up when you get in a real spot. I need someone I can trust all the way. It's down to you, buddy—don't make me beg. I'm really up against it."

"I suppose you crossed the wrong hombre this time?"

"You might say that—but it's not what you think."

"Try me."

Raskin moved to the bed and sat, dropping the envelope and a pile of ash on the comforter. His eyes did a circuit of the room, flitting from wall to wall, taking careful stock of the generic décor as if he'd never been in a hotel room before. He stared for a moment at the foxhunt lithograph over the bed: men in red coats leaping a hedgerow on horseback. Their doomed quarry fled with wild eyes toward the corner of the frame. Raskin's right foot began tapping out a brisk rhythm on the floor. The tapping did not seem conscious. The foot was off on its own. "You don't want to know," he said.

"Try me," Stucky repeated.

"It's for your own good," said Raskin, standing abruptly.

He crossed to the window and stood behind the curtain, peeking one eye around it to survey the street below. "See that car down there?"

Stucky looked. A white sedan stood at the curb nine stories down—a late-model import, he believed, a Nissan or Toyota. There were probably a billion such cars in the Los Angeles basin, circling the highways and byways like so many ants in a farm, indistinguishable from one another. A dark figure sat alone in the driver's seat.

"I suppose it followed you here."

"Wrong. If they knew I was here we'd have a certified shit show on our hands. With any luck, they think I'm dead. But they're tailing you just in case, get it?"

"Not even slightly. Whose body did the cops pull out of that fire?"

"The body was a black market special—mortician with a sidelight, that kind of thing. Kids in school and he needs the extra cash. Cadavers are a cinch to come by in this town, believe me. But really, bud, it's better if your knowledge stops there. Old Raskin's in a little over his head this time."

"I didn't know there was any 'over Raskin's head.'"

"One of the unpleasant things you learn too late in the game. Get back from the window."

Stucky got back from the window. Raskin pulled the curtain and struck a flamingo pose to stub his cigarette on the bottom of his shoe, nearly toppling over in the process. He flicked the butt in the general direction of the trash. "What I need from you is simple, Stuck."

"No doubt."

"It is." He lit another smoke and sucked it like the nozzle of nitric tank. "See that envelope?" He pointed at the bed. "All you have to do is hold it for me—just for a couple days."

"Hmm."

"That's it, bud, I swear. I'll contact you in a few days and tell you where to send it. Then you just drop 'er in the mail and forget the whole thing."

"And what if 'they' find out I'm holding it? I don't suppose 'they'll' be too gentle in their approach."

"They won't find out. How would they find out?"

"Well," Stucky said, "that's hard for me to figure, since I don't even know who the hell they are."

"OK, so you're a little scared. I understand. A man of letters, you don't like the rough stuff."

"I'm not scared. The point is not that I'm scared."

"No harm will come to you, Stuck. I personally guarantee it."

"Ha! A great relief. I'll call my insurance guy, he might

drop my premiums."

"Please, buddy. Just do this one thing for me and I'll never ask for your help again."

Stucky didn't answer. He didn't have to; they both knew the answer already. His protests were perfunctory, ceremonial, like the plot elements of a porn. He was a lonely, buxom housewife, Raskin the TV repairman.

"Oh, Christ. Does Nathalie know you're still alive?"

Raskin shook his head. "She can't know—whatever else happens, she can't know."

Stucky narrowed his eyes. "She deserves better than you."

"Right, well, don't they all. Three days, Stuck. No more. You just drop it in the mail." He tried the rakish grin again but couldn't hold it. He looked down and laughed, or made a sound that might have been laughter. It was, in spite of everything, unnerving to see Raskin in such a state.

"Oh, Christ. All right, fine. Three days, man. I'll wait to hear from you."

Raskin sighed. "Thanks, buddy. I knew I could count on you." He stepped forward and offered his hand. It was damp and cold to the touch. "You know," he said, lowering his voice, "I don't think I ever told you how much I admired *de Gaulle*. That scene where he kisses Pétain on the mouth in Bordeaux—it's truly affecting, Stuck. I couldn't get it out of my head for weeks. You've got the gift, buddy. These Hollywood leeches don't deserve you."

"Thanks, Raskin. Thank you. I didn't know you read books."

He looked Stucky dead in the eye. The cigarette smoldered in the corner of his mouth. "I read your book."

Perhaps Raskin wasn't so changeless after all. He winked and dropped Stucky's hand, but their eyes remained locked for a moment — Raskin's gray eyes shot with blood, tiny veins like winter branches snaking out from raw red rims. A smile seemed to pass behind them, or the shadow of a smile. An inward expression, distant and resigned. Raskin in his humble season? Raskin awash in the abasement of life? Raskin waltzes slowly with that bitter mistress, his mortality, to the threnodial sob of bagpipes? Stucky said, "How'd your horse do this afternoon?"

"Don't know. Didn't get to see. Vichy Dog in the fourth at Santa Anita — check tomorrow's paper."

"Vichy Dog?"

"A little nod to you, pal — and to *La Résistance*." The sad smile leaked out across his lips. "Take it easy." He moved to the door and paused with his hand on the knob. "One more thing," he said, turning halfway back around. "Don't open that envelope. Whatever you do, Stuck, don't read what's in there. For your own sake."

Stucky nodded. He raised a hand to wave his friend goodbye. Raskin opened the door, craned his neck outside, glanced quickly in either direction, and slipped into the hall.

Stucky tore the envelope open as soon the door swung shut. He was greatly surprised to find what appeared to be the manuscript of a novel inside: *Fauntleroy's Ghost* by Robert D. Raskin. So the title page announced, above the clip-art image of an old time movie camera silhouetted in profile. This was followed by two hundred and seventeen pages of densely packed prose: single-spaced, Times New Roman font. Stucky hefted the stack of paper in his hands, feeling its solid, novelistic weight — the weight, in his own life, of ruined dreams. A lump rose in histhroat. Watching a dead man emerge from his closet had brought no fear, but now he was afraid. Existential panic, the worst and most familiar kind — where had Raskin found the time to write a novel? Stucky sat down at the desk, turned with trepidation to the first page, and began to read:

Ernesto Fauntleroy. His name is like a joyride for the tongue, the syllables a legend unto themselves, rising and falling like the impetuous fortunes of men. I heard them first in Antwerp, on the lips of an Aussie who'd lost both his eyes smuggling stones from Côte d'Ivoire — lovely blue eyes, piercing, eyes that made women spend money. Or so he claimed. But then again, truth is just the name we hang on what dreams we need believe. Fauntleroy taught me that. This story is the truest one I know. "Ernesto Fauntleroy," the Aussie whispered, "are you familiar with his work? No? But tell me, mate, just tell me this: Do you like the movies?"

Fauntleroy, the manuscript explained, had been the greatest producer in Hollywood in the late '60's and '70's — a legend in the business, a reclusive genius, the driving force behind countless films, including such "classics" as *False Witness, Clay Pigeon*, and *Death's Little Sister*. He worked behind the scenes, tirelessly, ducking the limelight. No one knew where he'd come from, though he was a man to whom rumors attached, whispers of a sinister past. Then in 1985 he abruptly vanished back into the ether from which he'd emerged two decades before. Some said he was dead, some that he had fallen gravely ill, others that he'd simply retired, slipped away in secret to live out his healthy years in peace. Strange tropical diseases were mentioned, gradual disfigurement; also a ranch near Bolinas. Some predicted his eventual return, but it never happened. But of such more recent matters the blind Aussie knew little; his was a tale of the sinister past. He claimed to have met Fauntleroy before his Hollywood turn, when both were running guns through Mombasa in the late '50's. These were the salad days for resourceful men in Africa, the end of colonialism and the height of the Cold War. The continent was a vast patchwork of blood money and shifting allegiances; for those who learned to read the angles, opportunity was everywhere. Fauntleroy learned. He took chances no other man could stomach, said the Aussie, and never got caught on the wrong side—until Lumumba fell in the Congo. This was late 1960; Fauntleroy was down in Katanga province, in a hut amongst the copper mines, exploiting the chaos with his usual flair, arming both factions in the local separatist war. Then a squad of Belgian mercenaries captured him in March of '61 and should have killed him straight away, that would've been the normal thing. But they didn't. Fauntleroy talked his way out somehow, and back in Mombasa he wouldn't say how. But the Aussie had gradually developed a theory: he'd come to believe that Fauntleroy was in possession of the secret film of Patrice Lumumba's execution.

Lumumba, of course, had been a dreamer, a patriot, a rhetorical firebrand—a man born to political martyrdom like a fish to water, whether he knew it or not. He led the struggle for Congolese independence, became the nation's first Prime Minister, refused to play ball with the CIA, cozied up to Moscow for leverage, and got himself deposed in the Mobutu coup after just ten weeks in power. Then Mobutu sent him down to Katanga, where he was driven into the jungle and shot. Details of the event were murky. Rumors of a film circulated for years, and the footage was said to be explosive—but what did it show? Direct American involvement? Belgian troops pulling the trigger? A secret double-cross by the Soviets? A rogue faction from the UN? The Aussie wasn't sure, but he'd heard enough gossip to believe the film was real. If so, he reasoned, it would have been just like Fauntleroy to get his hands on such a thing, and the footage—or rather, the threat of its release—would have made the perfect bargaining chip with which to secure his freedom from the Belgians. But he would've been obliged to keep it, of course, as a guarantee on his life, and keeping it would've presented new dangers. What he would've needed was a place to hide the film in plain sight, a mode of concealment that wasn't concealed at all. It had taken the Aussie years of idle consideration before he realized how perfectly these facts dovetailed with Fauntleroy's disappearance from Africa later in '61 and his subsequent arrival on the Los Angeles scene. But once he saw it, the truth seemed blindingly obvious: Fauntleroy had gone to Hollywood to bury the Lumumba film; he'd become a producer to hide the film in his movies. Ten frames here, five more there, patiently scattered across the long breadth of his catalog in flashes so quick the viewer missed them at regular speed. The project took years, and when it was finished he disappeared again. But he'd left the footage behind, and whoever reassembled it would be able to name his price. The theory was so crazy it had to be true, the Aussie believed it with religious conviction. But he was blind, old, broken and broke—he needed a partner to do the legwork. He needed someone like Raskin's narrator, an investment man with money and the right connections, a man not unfamiliar with delicate jobs, who just happened to live in Los Angeles—a man, in other words, who sounded an awful lot like Robert D. Raskin himself.

That was just the setup.

A deal was struck at the close of Chapter Two; the plot galloped onward from there in Raskin's breathless prose. The whole thing was pure drivel, really, overwrought and with all the historical integrity of Stalin's falsified memoirs, though a certain cheap brio spurred the story along. Nonetheless, Stucky felt his eyelids going heavy somewhere in early Chapter Three. Crowded words swarmed across each page but he pressed on. The narrator—Dean Steel—returns to California to begin collecting prints of Fauntleroy's movies, and the Aussie's hunch seems to prove out: a small snatch of mysterious footage lurks somewhere in each film, cryptic images, difficult to parse. As Steel labors to assemble the puzzle, strange happenings commence. He finds himself pursued by shadowy figures, tailed by unmarked cars, warned by roughnecks to drop his quest. His house is ransacked; the Aussie disappears. Paranoia descends, gripping the prose itself—but was this literary artifice, consciously deployed to convey Steel's mounting anxiety, or a dark window into the author's own psychosis? Stucky fell asleep before the end. He woke up sweating in his chair, buzzed by the sense of vivid dreams he could not quite recall. The phone was ringing. Sunlight leaked around the edges of his curtain; the hotel operator was chewing gum. Stucky could hear her snapping the wad. "This is your wake-up call," she said. *Snap snap.*

He placed the receiver back on the hook. Raskin's novel lay before him on the desk. He stuffed it back into its envelope and dropped the envelope into the top desk drawer. There was a handwritten note on the backside, beside the clasp, a single line scrawled in red ballpoint ink: *39 Calle Sinaloa, 2/23, 10 pm-?* February 23rd was today. Stucky copied the address onto a slip of hotel notepaper and closed the drawer. He slipped the notepaper into his pocket and stood. A light tingle as the blood returned to his haunches. He stepped to the window and pulled the curtain back. The sky outside burned blue like Nathalie's eyes, almost. Stucky was expected in Burbank.

"I was attacked by a dog," Jack Zweller said.

He stared down gravely at his left hand sheathed in a black glove with the fingertips cut away. The rest of his wide body was encased in a gray cotton tracksuit; sunlight capered across his sweating pate, bald on top beneath a comb-over. Jack Zweller, independent producer of films—Stucky considered him considering the hand. They sat on folding chairs at a card table on the concrete patio behind Zweller's Burbank office building. The swish of passing traffic out on Victory Boulevard flanked the building to reach their ears.

"A golden retriever?" Stucky guessed.

"Fuck a golden retriever—I should be so lucky. We're talking German shepherd. Nazi cop dog, bred to chew the flesh of innocents. I'm out walking in my neighborhood one morning when I see it watching me from across the street. There's no one else around, just the two of us, and I mean this thing stares dead at me—straight into my goddamn eyes. I mean there was *communication* in this look. Feelings and ideas. Some people think an animal like that is dumb. Not so. It's dumb for higher math but what the hell, so am I—probably you too. Writing scripts ain't splitting the atom. A dog like that is a genius for the primal stuff. It wants a piece of my ass—that's what the look says. A whole history of warfare in the look. Primitive struggle, dingoes on the veldt. I don't wait for the high sign, I take off at a sprint."

"But I guess the dog was faster."

"Well, I don't know. Ran ten feet and got hit by a car. Shattered my elbow into sixty-seven pieces, two of which the docs never even found." He flexed his left forearm and moved it slowly up and down, rotating the damaged joint. The elbow clicked and clacked like an old wooden rollercoaster beneath the gray fabric. "This is a pressure glove. Not sure what the hell it's supposed to do but the docs say wear it, so I wear it. Someday they'll say stop but if they ever nix my Demerol I'll murder their children."

Stucky grinned. He was in fine spirits despite his strange evening and short, upright sleep. Mild euphoria like a feather tickling his brain. "So what happened to the dog?"

"I don't know, fuck the dog—maybe the dog never existed, maybe I made the son of a bitch up. Wouldn't be the first time. The point is the look he gave me. Communication of the primal. That look was a film in itself. Eat, fuck, kill—these are the basics, what anyone can relate to. That's the stuff to make movies about. Anyway, let's hear about yours."

Zweller sat back, ceding the floor. Above the glove and tracksuit he wore a beard that grew in silver patches on his doughy cheeks and neck. His face was pale outside its Rudolphy nose, a bulbous structure trimmed with burst capillaries.

Stucky grinned wider and cleared his throat. Perhaps he would emphasize the dramatic virtues of his screenplay's closing act. Running through his plot points as quickly as possible, he arrived at the penultimate scene and paused to underscore the simmering tension.

"Mexico City, summer 1940..."

Trotsky sips tea in the house at Coyoacán. Bitter quarrel with Rivera the year before; Trotsky rents his own rooms now. Why must everything end in discord? Because, Trotsky thinks: history. The world is at war again. Ostensibly the issues are many, but in truth a single issue pertains. The workers cannot fail (again) to see the folly of slaughtering each on end for the ends of their oppressors. Truth will out, the moment will come—Trotsky will be called. His trust is with the people but so few people remain for him to trust. Are the bodyguards loyal? The secretaries? He stands from the table and strolls outside. Geraniums and roses adorn the patio in generous shades of purple and red. A flower garden is a bourgeois pleasure, but is the beauty of a flower subject to the foibles of class? Chickens discourse in their coops of wood and wire; rabbits in their classless warrens mate with rabbit zeal.

A thing cannot be else but what it is. Trotsky is a revolutionary, but also a man of sixty. He is tired. Stalin's thugs riddled the house with bullets in May; August lies now like a mellow song across the Valley of the Damned. Jacson arrives to discuss the future of Trotsky's ideas in Canada, bearing a manuscript for Trotsky's critique. In the study, Trotsky bends at the desk to read. Jacson draws an ice axe from beneath his raincoat and drives it into the old man's skull. Trotsky turns, spits on his attacker, bites his hand. Jacson carries a pistol and dagger besides the alpine tool, but Trotsky—though thirty years his senior— wrestles him to the ground. The bodyguards rush in, set upon Jacson and mean to kill him—but Trotsky stays their blows. "Stop!" he orders. "This man has a story to tell!"

But what is Trotsky's story in the end? He reclines on the kitchen floor, covered like history in blood. Dying in a Green Cross hospital the next day, as Jacson recuperates in a room across the hall, he will dictate his final message, urging his followers to go forward, avowing his certainty of the Fourth International's success. These are the parting words of the world historical figure, but what does the man himself believe? He has lived and now died in the cause of rigid, high-flown ideals, but his path has been blocked at every turn by human weakness and chicanery—the very forces his theoretical frame- work seeks to disregard. What is the society of man, after all, but a vast conspiracy against the pure of heart? Is Trotsky a casualty of his own naïve refusal to grasp this fact—or has he, like Jesus, in fact grasped it perfectly from the start? The camera zooms in on his face framed by the hospital pillow: the quack doctor's beard and wild shock of hair above, the great burning fire in his eyes. Mexico's fierce summer light falls through the window and Trotsky turns to it, turns to it, opening his mouth as if to speak again. As a child in Yanovka, he once rode a dun-colored pony so far across the freshly ploughed fields...

Fade out.

Stucky stopped talking. A motorist on Victory Boulevard depressed his horn. Zweller nodded, once; he made an uncertain noise in his throat. He waited a moment and then leaned forward. He placed his right elbow on the card table's vinyl surface and wiped a sheet of sweat from his brow, squinting off to the right, where the traffic sounds wandered around the building's edge. His voice, when he spoke, was not unkind.

He said, "You don't get out to the movies very often, do you, Ben?"

No, Stucky did not go very often to the movies. He some-times rented older films from Captain Video on 15th Avenue— the last place on Capitol Hill still carrying VHS—but to the Cineplex he did not routinely go. He tended not to like new movies. But he'd been hoping no such inconvenient detail would keep him from successfully writing one—an impractical notion, maybe, but Stucky had a certain weakness for impractical notions. Unfortunately, fate maintained a bias against impractical men, as Trotsky had discovered or at least proven at the business end of an ice axe. Twenty years later, Patrice Lumumba proved it again; Stucky had written a paper in college about his ouster. Lashed to a rubber tree, facing down the muzzles of a firing squad, Lumumba might well have considered the value of practicality. He must have understood by then that righteousness is an ephemeral mandate without the support of the army. You can stump for truth and justice all the livelong post-colonial day, but misread the proxy politics and they'll never find your body. This was 1960, after all. Ike was sprinkling nukes around Turkey like baby powder on a newborn's crotch, while Khrushchev stewed, casting his pickled gaze towards Havana. The CIA was painting morality in the broadest possible strokes; they weren't about to take a flyer on some populist wunderkind commanding the wealth of central Africa. Lumumba tried to play the middle but there was no middle. He wanted to maintain his independence, but that wasn't one of the options. He was a great thinker but missed the central fact. Stucky could almost see the footage: grainy, the camera wobbles up and down, figures in a jungle clearing washed in the pale headlights of a Jeep. The gunshots are like firecrackers, like dry sticks snapping underfoot.

He would never sell his script. He stood on the sidewalk outside Zweller's office in the sun, watching the cars glide past. Down the street, a white Nissan sedan sat in one of the metered spots at the curb. The car was empty; a man stood smoking by a lamppost twenty or thirty feet away. He did not look in Stucky's direction. Where would Raskin be right now? Chasing down the prerogatives of his private baroque fantasy? Locked in some villain's basement, tied to a chair? He might be in Mazatlán already, he might be tanning in Cancun. Stucky removed from his pocket and once again examined the scrap of paper on which he'd scrawled the mysterious address from the back of Raskin's envelope. Whatever would happen there didn't begin till ten o'clock. That gave Stucky the whole day to kill.

He closed his eyes. The sun felt good on his skin. At thirty-six years old his career was over and he'd be broke in two months flat, but these facts seemed for the moment not to bind him. Everything depends on perspective, and perspective depends largely on the weather. In Seattle, under low clouds and the inevitable winter rain, he might have been forced to string a noose up over the shower rod. But in Burbank the sunlight fell grandly onto the broad window of a bar across Victory Boulevard, and Stucky gamely forded the traffic. It was, as they say, five o'clock somewhere. The time to flog his liver had arrived.

Calle Sinaloa turned out to be a narrow, winding lane in the Hollywood Hills, not far below the reservoir. Stucky negotiated the twists and turns with great care, the rental less than steady in his charge, following the street numbers as they counted down to a dead end packed with cars. Someone was having a party. Stucky double-parked and stepped out into the fine night air. Clean smell of eucalyptus and night-flowering jasmine up here above the city. Lights from the basin peered up between the houses; the breeze came up and set a bird of paradise to nodding, oral erotically. Stucky followed a pair of sharp-dressed couples toward the last house on the downhill side of the street. The women trailed sandalwood perfume across a flower garden and through the open front door—beside which two mosaic tiles displayed the numbers *3* and *9*.

The foyer into which they entered gave onto a wide

living room stretched along a picture widow, beyond which a deck overlooked the city. Guests had scattered themselves across couches and chairs, chatting at the amiable frequency of mid-party banter above the speaker-borne strains of Monk's piano: comely and successful people gathering in tasteful costume for ritual improvisations of wit and charm. A monkey-jacketed waiter approached to offer Stucky a glass of rosé. He might have been the twin of their barkeep from the Santa Monica Boulevard dive. Imagine a city of millions where every garçon has the jaw-line of Burt Lancaster. Stucky took the wine and turned to find Nathalie smiling at him from a doorway to his left.

"Ben!"

Stucky smiled back; her presence seemed almost like a thing he'd been expecting. Moving nimbly on three-inch heels, she crossed the carpet as the sound of church bells crosses a valley of freshly hayed fields. She wore a blue satin dress printed with samurai warriors; matching strings of topaz dangled from her delicate ears. One of them brushed Stucky's lips as she leaned in to kiss his cheek. Her blond hair smelled lightly of the sun.

"In Japan," Stucky said, "a woman's traditional period of mourning goes for two full years."

Nathalie laughed. "Patriarchal bullshit, don't you think? In Japan you can buy the panties of an underage girl from public vending machines." Her face took on a pensive cast. "I thought about it today. I thought, What would Bobby be doing tonight if I'd been the one who died in that fire?"

"Sailing for Cabo, no doubt, with his cock in the mouth of some sorority harlot from USC."

"Exactly. And that's what I loved about him."

"Well, then," Stucky said, lifting his glass, "let us not dishonor the dead."

Nathalie arched a single eyebrow. "My thoughts exactly." She reached back, plucked a full glass of red from the tray of a passing waiter, and raised it to meet Stucky's in the air.

"Boom," Stucky said.

They drank.

Nathalie looked away. "I almost called you today, Ben. All bluster aside, I've had better mornings. I'm not as strong as Bobby, really. I've been drinking since lunch."

"Me too. You hold it well for a girl your size."

"Practice makes perfect—but I almost drove into a palm tree on the way up here."

"So did I. The palm trees come out of nowhere in this town. We'll carpool on the way home and you can be my spotter."

"A chivalrous offer, but I'm planning to be incoherent by then. Anyway, what's your excuse? Something tells me it's more than crushing grief for Bobby."

"I'm a sensitive writer and Raskin was a very dear friend," Stucky said. "Don't lowball my empathy."

She narrowed her fabulous eyes. "If you don't highball my credulity, Shakespeare."

Stucky drained his glass and ditched it in a potted fern. "Did somebody say highball?"

Nathalie led him to a wet bar, unmanned, on the far side of the living room. A glittering array of pricey handles graced the bar top. Stucky poured the scotch with a limber arm. Fabulous indulgence to drink the good stuff when he could barely taste it. He'd played darts in Burbank for half the afternoon with a jug-eared man who claimed to train primates for television and film. Orangutans, the man alleged, could be taught to masturbate a human male, but with monkeys and chimps such games should never be played. Those were his exact words: "such games should never be played." A preposterous contention — but who even cared if it were true? In some crucial way, though perhaps not the traditional one, Stucky knew that it was. He topped off his glass and turned to survey the crowd.

"So who do you know here?"

Nathalie shrugged. "Who don't I know here? This town's the size of a snow-globe. What about you?"

"Well," Stucky said. Just then Bunsen came in from the deck. He caught sight of Stucky, gave him a friendly wave, and stumbled off down the hall. Stucky waved back. "I know Bunsen. He's considering my script for New Line."

"You never did get around to telling me about your script yesterday."

"Oh, I'd hate to bore you."

"Don't be coy, Ben. I'm sure it's not boring."

Stucky chuckled and worked the scotch. "How sure?"

"Try me."

The liquor was mellow in his throat; his brain seemed to float in its warmth. He looked down at her looking up at him over the rim of her glass. Even aboard the big heels she was short. A compact package — bite-sized, one might say. The blue satin of her dress went nicely with the neon sapphire of her eyes. Her little Joker's mouth was indeed beguiling. *Try me*, she said.

"OK. What do you know about Patrice Lumumba?"

"Patrice Lumumba?"

"That's right, Patrice Lumumba—the martyred father of Congolese independence."

"The name rings a bell, I guess. That's about it."

Just as Stucky had suspected. He smiled. "Come outside," he said. "I'll tell you everything."

He tucked the bottle of scotch under his arm and took her by the hand—a small hand, warm in his, thrilling heat of the flesh—weaving through the partygoers to the sliding door, and out into the cool winter air. The coolness was refreshing; the sky was clear and a bright winter moon shone down on the city. A moonlit blimp hovered over the clustered skyscrapers of downtown. He told her everything: the blind Aussie diamond pirate, the legendary lost Lumumba film, its potential implications, the mysterious Hollywood producer into whose hands it may or may not have fallen, his alleged scheme to conceal the footage in plain sight, and the courageous hero who will risk everything to find the truth—though in Stucky's version Steel is a man of letters, a novelist cum screenwriter bearing precious little resemblance to Raskin. He described the web of intrigue that deepens as Steel compiles the Lumumba frames, the powerful forces arrayed against him, in the face of which he tenaciously perseveres. A car chase, a ransacked home, thugs who issue cryptic threats. Stucky pulled on the scotch and watched the blimp ply its bovine arc out to sea.

"So how does it end?" Nathalie asked.

She was standing very close to him now. Stucky had read only half of Raskin's novel and could summon no idea for its denouement. He reached out, touched her arm.

"You'll just have to see the movie."

"You tease," she scolded. "Are you always such a tease, Ben Stucky?"

"No."

She nodded, solemnly. "I would love to see that movie. It's going to be wonderful."

"I hope so."

"It is, it's an amazing premise—really, Ben." She rubbed his arm and turned to lean back against the railing; Stucky turned too. He was close enough to breathe the clean smell of her hair again. "Ben Stucky from Seattle. Bobby always told me you were the smart one. How did you ever come up with the idea for that script?"

"It took me years," Stucky said.

The party seemed a little more crowded now. The sliding door was closed but a thumping bass beat floated out from the living room. Jack Zweller was mixing himself a drink at the bar. He glanced up and grinned at Stucky through the window, tipping an imaginary cap with his gloved left hand.

"You know Zweller too?"

"Sure. He loves my script. He's dying to produce it."

"I bet he is. There's so much crap out there. He was telling us before you got here about some poor schmo he met this morning who's trying to shop a bio-pic about Leon Trotsky, for god's sake."

"Ha," Stucky said.

"So what's your movie called?"

"*Fauntleroy's Ghost.*"

Nathalie stiffened, lifting her eyes. "Fauntleroy? Why

Fauntleroy?"

"That's the producer's name—the one who hides the Lumumba film. Ernesto Fauntleroy."

A brief silence fell between them. On the living room carpet, languid women moved to the beat.

"But Ernesto Fauntleroy owns this house," Nathalie said. "Ernesto Fauntleroy is our host tonight."

Stucky blinked. He considered this fact, or tried to consider it. The information seemed to have no place in his files. Through the glass, women dancing, languid, wired like puppets to the bass. Stucky pasted on a smile. The bass hopped around inside his ears. "Exactly," he managed to say.

"But do you know him?"

"No one really knows him," Stucky whispered.

"That's true," she whispered back. "No one had even seen him for twenty years until a few weeks ago. I heard he was living on an ashram somewhere, or that he joined a monastery in Tibet."

"Tibet he did," Stucky breathed. "I heard that one myself."

She put her mouth against his ear—warm breath, moist inside his aural canal. "Some say he's crazy."

"People say all kinds of things about Fauntleroy. That's why I made him the focus of my script."

"But you even used his real name."

"The name is part of his mystique."

"Yes, I suppose it is."

Silence again; Stucky tried again to think. Difficult business. His sozzled thoughts drifted like a flock of crewless blimps. Ernesto Fauntleroy owned this house. Light fell from the living room of Ernesto Fauntleroy in a pale sheet onto his deck. The breeze resumed, tickling brittle eucalyptus leaves as it came up the hill. Stucky felt its cool breath play across the back of his neck.

"I guess you came here to meet him tonight."

"I—" He looked away. "I don't know why I came here."

"There's no reason to be shy, Ben. Would you like me to introduce you?"

Stucky didn't answer. He didn't know the answer. Nathalie took hold of his wrist and towed him back through the sliding door, back into the living room. She parked him beside a metal floor lamp and said, "Wait here. I'll go find Ernesto Fauntleroy."

Stucky nodded. Dog-like obedience: he would wait. She walked away, shifting tastily under her dress. Stucky conferred with the scotch. The living room air seemed warm and dense, the music not so loud as he'd thought from outside. Ernesto Fauntleroy was their host tonight. All around, people were talking. Their voices swirled, yielding shards of broken thought, scraps of butchered pitch and tone. On a nearby couch, Bunsen thumb-wrestled an elegant redhead with big hands. There seemed to be no flirtation in the contest; their faces were tense, fixed on the battle: thrust and retreat, thrust and retreat. Behind them, in the foyer, a pretty young Latina stood talking on her phone. Stucky knew her at once. Her smile bespoke a pleasant conversation, perhaps with a lover or some longtime friend, but her ferret struggled wildly against its taut leash on the floor—straining, it seemed, to come forth and give Stucky a warning. The general volume of chatter rose as Nathalie emerged from the hallway with what appeared to be a very old man on her arm.

"Is that him?" someone asked.

"There he is!"

"Is that Fauntleroy?"

"It must be, but..."

"My god, he looks so..."

"...some terrible disease..."

"...but Redford always said he was the best."

"Jesus, get a load of his face."

He had no face. His head was swaddled like a mummy, wrapped from crown to collar in layered strips of hospital gauze, the face entirely obscured. He sported a pair of gold-rimmed aviator shades atop the bandages, and below this, a button-up khaki jacket with matching pants, accented by an ascot the color of fresh blood. His shoes were burnished alligator, his posture badly stooped; his claw-like left hand clutched Nathalie's forearm with geriatric intensity, the ancient fear of broken hips. They advanced at a slow shuffle, beset by a line of guests stepping forward to offer their hands. The masked man shook each one politely, adding perhaps a nod or passing phrase. In his mouth — a dark hole in the gauze — he held the largest cigar Stucky had ever seen.

"Christ, that's creepy."

"What kind of..."

"Brando always worshipped him, of course."

"Fauntleroy!"

Stucky eyed his approach with a slack jaw, neck

craned forward, squinting as if to read fine print. He tried to scrutinize the crumpled figure: his gauze-wrapped head, his frail bearing... Raskin? The faceless man was roughly Raskin's height, within range, perhaps, of Raskin's diminished build — and yet he tottered like a genuine geezer; he seemed to move toward Stucky like a figure in a dream. Even at a distance, his hands were plainly flecked with liver spots and streaked with purple veins — which might, in theory, be nothing more than stage makeup. The fingers sank like talons into Nathalie's skin. Stucky searched her face for a clue. Her grin was broad, inscrutable, both inviting and carnivorous at once. Her eyes glowed no less blue from half a room away. They fell on Stucky and executed a deft, cinematic wink — meaning what, exactly? He tried to wink back but it came out more like a Tourettic facial tic. He downed another jolt of scotch, stood swaying lightly on his feet, and waited.

"Ben," she said when they reached him. "Ben? I have someone very special here for you to meet."

She turned to her companion but he did not speak straight away. He seemed, behind his mask, to size Stucky up like a cattleman at auction. He removed the prodigious cigar from his mouth and tapped a ring of ash onto the floor.

"Hello. Our friend Nathalie informs me that you are the finest young writer in all of Hollywood. Welcome to my home. I am Ernesto Fauntleroy."

His voice was rasping but faintly melodic, touched by a nameless accent. Stucky shook his hand and it returned no pressure: slack skin, dry as snake molt. The bandages looked fresh — expertly applied, fastened by steel clips, tented at the nose.

But no part of the nose was visible; the eyes lay hidden behind their mirrored shades. Even his lips were covered—though when he smiled, as he seemed to be smiling now, two rows of crooked, yellow, possibly false teeth came into view.

"Ben Stucky," Stucky said.

"So you are. It's a pleasure to make your acquaintance. I've always enjoyed the acquaintance of writers. Actors I find insufferable, for the most part, and directors are even worse—but writers, Mr. Stucky, I have always enjoyed."

A chorus of chuckles from the nearest bystanders. Stucky was aware of their bodies pressing closer as they strained to hear. Fauntleroy's presence seemed to focus the room's scattered gravity.

"Yes," Stucky said, "writers are terrific." His eyes combed the bandages, the shades, the entire blank mug. "Writers are the tits."

"Indeed. Is everything all right, Mr. Stucky?"

"Sure, sure."

"I do hope you'll excuse my dreadful appearance this evening. It is my misfortune to suffer from a rare condition of the skin. Extremely painful. But less so tonight, I'm pleased to say, for the sight of so many good friends, old and new alike." He spread his lipless, yellow-tooth grin.

Stucky studied the teeth. "What kind of skin condition?"

"Ben," said Nathalie, "I hope you won't mind, but I told Mr. Fauntleroy about your script. I just told him a little, but he thinks it sounds *fascinating*. Isn't that right, Mr. Fauntleroy?"

"Yes, quite so. Entirely fascinating—a fascinating choice of subject, to say the least. I see you have a drink already, Mr.

Stucky. May I offer you a cigar?"

Stucky looked down at the bottle still in his hand. Not much left. The sight of its emptiness seemed instantly to make him drunker; the challenge to his powers of discernment was manifest. He took the fresh cigar without a word and examined it carefully: eight inches long, already cut, its wrapper smelling damply of the good earth — smelling almost like a woman. He pressed the dark leaf against his nose and drew a long breath.

"Here," said Nathalie.

She produced a lighter and struck the flame. Stucky leaned down to accept it — a bluntly sexual transaction; he seemed to feel the heat of Fauntleroy's stare, and beyond him the eyes of the crowd. The room had quieted considerably. Stucky took a few slow puffs, turning the cigar end in a circle in the lighter flame. Rich smoke filled his mouth. He held it for a moment, then exhaled.

"Wonderful," he announced.

Fauntleroy nodded. "A Cohiba Lancero, Laguito #1. I first discovered them in 1977, when we were shooting *¡Viva la Tropicana!* in Havana — not an easy thing to arrange in those days, believe me. But Castro had drained his coffers in Angola and Ethiopia, and Brezhnev couldn't pick the slack up anymore, he had problems of his own. I was blessed with certain connections, channels of communication that were open to me. Castro needed money and we had to have the location, it was indispensable to the film. I saw the opportunity and brokered a deal — a good deal for everyone, I daresay, but that didn't mean Fidel had to like it..."

He paused. Long, indulgent puffs. His mouth hole sent up clouds of gauzy smoke. Someone had killed the music.

"He summoned me to a meeting our first night in town, Mr. Stucky. Soldiers shook me out of bed and took me by jeep to a compound west of the city, where he was having dinner—alone at a cement table with a boliche roast the size of your arm and a gallon of buffalo milk, both of which he offered to share. Of course I accepted. The meat was delicious. He described for me his theories about the effects of buffalo milk on male potency— a robust man, charismatic and imposing, six-foot-five at least. The kind of man who makes a revolution with his hands. After dinner he presented me with a case of these very cigars. They weren't even publicly available in Havana at the time, Cohiba was Castro's personal brand. Of course I was obliged to thank him, but he waved me off. I want you to enjoy your stay, he said, and I would like you to think of me for as long as you remain in my country. These are the finest cigars in the world. Each time you light one, I want you to remember Fidel. Then he stood up and unzipped his pants. He took out his member and dropped it on the table beside one of the cigars. They were exactly the same length. He was limp, and his girth was far greater, but their length was the same. He stood with his arms crossed and allowed me to have a good look. Then he sat back down and wished me the best of luck with my film, and that was the end of our meeting."

Stucky took the cigar from his mouth and considered its tremendous size again. Somewhere behind him, a woman groaned. "Well." He burped, softly but not on purpose. "So much for Freud, I guess."

Fauntleroy chuckled. A ripple of laughter ran through the room, as if on his cue. Stucky glanced at Nathalie and tried again to read her enigmatic smile.

"Of course it was a warning, Mr. Stucky, and not even a hostile one, but rather a dispassionate expression of the realities at hand, a reminder to construe my business narrowly and stick to it—less for his good, really, than for my own. I was, after all, playing on his turf. I may regard myself as a clever man and perhaps I am; I may have achieved a certain degree of success in my life, but I am not Castro—not in Havana, at least. Ultimately, had I intended any manner of foolishness, I would have been no more than a gnat buzzing round his head, he could have crushed me with a slap whenever chose. He simply wished to ensure that I understood this. He was, in other words, doing me a favor. His method was gentle but the terms were clear as day." Fauntleroy leaned closer, dropping his voice. "Do you understand why I'm sharing this with you, Mr. Stucky?"

Stucky blanched. "Yes, I think so. I do."

"I deplore violence, Mr. Stucky. At my age, one learns to deplore violence."

Stucky wagged his head up and down in agreement. Their faces were just inches apart. Dense smells of tobacco and cologne—but nothing medicinal, no odors of the nursing home, no reek of rotting flesh. Stucky recalled Raskin's breezy voice on the phone a week before, unmarred by the lilt of any strange accent: *fossil Jews, old Havana, I watch them light cigars on the terrace—beautiful Cohibas, they never run out.*

"Good. I'm glad we understand each other."

"Yes," Stucky said.

Fauntleroy stepped back, returning his voice to a normal volume. "Then let us relax and enjoy ourselves this evening. Ladies and gentlemen, I've taken the liberty of inviting for your entertainment a very special guest with whom I believe many of you will already be familiar. Mr. Johansen?" he called. "Mr. Johansen? Bring out Walter!"

Everyone whooped and applauded; the promise of Walter seemed to excite them. Stucky applauded too, beating his hands together in a daze. His friend the primate trainer entered through the kitchen door with an orange-haired orangutan in tow. The orangutan waddled—or perhaps moseyed—with his belly thrust forward, knuckles dragging on the carpet. He was dressed like Howdy Doody, in a fringed cowboy shirt and straw Stetson; a plastic gun belt encircled his waist. The jug-eared trainer did not look Stucky's way as he explained that Walter had been working up some new material for his impending role in "Rosie O'Shea's Wild West Revue" at Universal Studios. The ape then produced a harmonica from his shirt pocket and began a faltering, discordant instrumental rendition of "Home on the Range."

Oh, give me a home where the buffalo roam...

Stucky felt his mouth go slack again. Air moved in and out. He watched in stunned silence as Walter's meaty lips slobbered the harp. Though really it made perfect sense: the tuneless notes, or perhaps the fact of who was playing them, merely echoed the dark promise fate had been whispering in his ear for the past two days. The trainer—Johansen—stood aside, regarding his charge's performance with a possessive, possibly carnal intensity. Several members of the audience raised their voices to softly intone the chorus: *Where never is heard a discouraging word, and the skies are not cloudy all day...*

As Stucky listened, his scrim of confusion seemed to lift. It seemed to burn away like the previous morning's sea fog. The proper perspective included, for example, Walter—who pressed on, mangling the second verse, to which no one sounded very sure of the words. Stucky polished off the scotch; the empty bottle slipped from his fingers and dropped harmlessly to the carpet below. The room teetered lengthwise along its axis— port to starboard, starboard to port—and he turned back to Fauntleroy, who stood puffing grandly on his Cohiba. His wrinkly hand still rested on Nathalie's forearm, but he was petting it now like the head of a cat—Stucky watched the fingers stroking spryly back and forth. They didn't move like the digits of any doddering oldster.

"Raskin," Stucky hissed under his breath.

How could he have doubted it? For reasons that might remain forever nameless—that might not even exist—Raskin was playing him again. As the swallows return to Capistrano, as a river returns to the sea, thus did Raskin take advantage of his friends. The goal of the scheme hardly mattered; for Raskin, as for any great conman, the scheme was a goal unto itself. If the scheme demanded the issuance of veiled threats to Stucky via Castro's leviathan dong, so be it. Stucky's pride, his years of loyal friendship, the general fragility of his psyche at a trying moment in his life—none of these would be considerations. Raskin's elegance was all surface. In his chest beat the heart of a barbarian. He'd been making a monkey of Stucky for nearly two decades now—but with a desperate man such games should never be played. Walter reached his closing note and the crowd burst into a rousing ovation. In the moment of silence that followed, Stucky found himself stepping forward, somewhat unsteadily, to reclaim the attention of the room.

"Thank you, Walter, that was beautiful. A lovely song. But you know, it's funny—your little story just reminded me of something, Mr. Fauntleroy. Reminded me of another story. Also involves Communists. Would you like to hear it?"

There was an awkward pause. Everyone looked at Stucky, then turned to look at their host, who shook his mummified head. "No, Mr. Stucky, I would not."

"Fascinating bunch, those Communists. You know much about the October Revolution, Mr. Fauntleroy? 1918? No? Then maybe you don't know that Lenin kept himself holed up for most of it at Bolshevik headquarters in the Smolny Institute—the Smolny Institute for Noble Maidens, that is. Old finishing school for rich girls. Aristocratic trim, as you might say. He rarely went down to the street. Risky down there, Karensky's men out looking for him and what not. But when he did have to go, he always made sure to disguise himself. Had a big gray wig, top of the line, from the costume guy at the Maryinsky Theater, and funny glasses—and sometimes he wore surgical bandages. Yes: surgical bandages. Trotsky writes about it in his memoirs." Stucky wrote about it in his script. Smolny, 25 October: Trotsky and Lenin at rest in a vacant room, waiting for the Second Congress of the Soviets to open. The pace of events has been giddy; Trotsky himself is a trifle giddy. Who stood last night in the cold atop the routed Tsar's Packard, exhorting a crowd of thousands in the street? Trotsky did. Now he lies beside Lenin in the dark on a blanket brought by Ilych's sister, but neither man can sleep. Petrograd is all but theirs. Twenty years of struggle—with and often against each other— and now their time has suddenly come. Trotsky turns to make a wistful remark about the naval garrison at Kronstadt, but instead begins laughing, he is laughing—Lenin's silhouette still wears enormous glasses, a cheap workman's cap, and bandages around the jaw as if to dress a toothache; he's neglected in the rush of things to remove his afternoon's disguise! "Lev Davidovich," he asks, "why are you laughing?" But Ilych now is laughing, too; they are laughing together. History lies prone at their feet—and Trotsky, whose uncompromising nature has so often left him lonely, has finally made for himself a wonderful friend. Stucky said, "Do you understand why I'm sharing this with you, *Mr. Fauntleroy*?"

"Because you're drunk, Mr. Stucky?"

"Try again."

"I think you'd better leave."

"This man is an imposter," Stucky announced.

The crowd absorbed this news in silence.

"This man is an imposter. He is perpetrating a fraud."

Someone in the back coughed. Comely faces, many still tan despite the season, either stared at Stucky quizzically or pointedly did not.

"He's not who he says—not who he says he is!"

"You tell 'em, Comrade!" Zweller shouted from the bar.

Nathalie came forward, put a hand on Stucky's shoulder. "Ben?"

He cut his eyes at her. Seductive features, sympathetically arranged—perfidy failed to spoil her looks. Beauty: not a moral force. She spoke to him as one speaks to calm a dog.

"We've had a lot to drink, Ben. I think you're confused."

"Fraud!" he called over her head.

People looked away now. Even Walter looked away, scratching the top of his hairy head with the edge of his harmonica. Here and there, a stifled laugh. Stucky felt the blood hammering behind his face. The alleged Fauntelroy had taken a few shuffle-steps backward at his shambling faux-elderly pace; he raised one of his liver-splotched faux-elderly hands and a pair of large men in dark suits stepped forward.

"Look under the bandages, you fools! He's just a man!"

One of the suits said, "There's two ways we can do this, Mr. Stucky."

Stucky regarded them coolly: broad shoulders, square, neckless heads. His breath was coming heavily now. Nathalie, too, had moved away.

The other one said, "The choice is up to you."

Drunks the world over are feared for their astounding strength. Stucky could feel the power. His anger was cumulative, aged like the scotch, also buttressed by it. He felt his body spring before it sprang: felt the room blur as he flew forward, tearing the stupid bandages from Raskin's face, exposing him for all to see—the collective gasp of the crowd, outraged cries, Stucky, triumphant, holding the gauze aloft... but he took no more than a step before the suits corralled him. Hands like ancient limestone made light of his struggles. They lifted him off the ground. His body was weightless, he was floating. They carried him doorward through a roomful of his crazed and shouting voice.

"Raskin! You bastard! You're a shitty writer! Your prose is garbage! Let go of me! Let go of me!"

He woke in the morning at the helm of his rental car on a side street in the Hollywood flats. His cheek lay flat against the cold leatherette of the steering wheel and he was drooling, or at least he had been, though his mouth seemed now to be out of saliva. He lifted his head. It bobbled precariously but did not fall off. The steering wheel's pebbled grain lay printed on his cheek; a scratch of unknown provenance marked his brow. The street before him was empty and the harsh early light made it look emptier. Traffic flowed past at the intersection up ahead, vehicles moving at incredible speeds. Stucky was pleased to find his key in the ignition. He turned it and the radio sprang an ambush, volume cranked to high—some morning talk show host yelling about whales: "Whales!" Stucky turned the car off. He adjusted the radio dial and tried again. At the intersection he turned left onto Hollywood Boulevard, away from the sun, and drove until he hit Fairfax, until he hit Sunset, until he hit the 405. Heading south on the freeway, he passed the Wilshire exit and kept going. He would call the hotel later. He would have them ship his bag.

At the airport he sat before the window at an empty gate and forced himself to finish a thirty-two-ounce bottle of water. The water was cold and clear, with a line of snow-capped peaks along the label, but it tasted exactly like scotch. Out across the runwayed concrete, planes diagonally rose and fell. The light mellowed slightly as the sun climbed higher in the hazy inland sky; ear-muffed baggage handlers gathered their shortening shadows in. Stucky stood to throw his empty bottle away. A rifled newspaper lay beside the trashcan on the floor: yesterday's *L.A. Times.* He picked it up and extracted the sports page. The Lakers had won; the Clippers had lost; the Dodgers had re-signed their shortstop to a lucrative long-term deal. Stucky hesitated for a moment before flipping to the track results, which revealed that no horse by the name of Vichy Dog had gone to the post for Wednesday's fourth at Santa Anita. A gelding named Fireside Surprise had won the race, paying six dollars even. Stucky looked out the window again.

His flight didn't leave for three more hours. Soon, in the timeless tradition of Los Angeles, it would be a lovely day. A slow parade of commuter jets taxied by, nose to tail like a train of circus bears, before alighting one by one out toward the Pacific. Fifteen hundred miles to the south, in Coyoacán, in the court-yard where he had once tended rabbits, Trotsky's bones lay moldering beneath a concrete obelisk that bore no epitaph, just a hammer and sickle and Trotsky's famous name. Which wasn't even really his — it had belonged originally to a handsome warder at the Odessa prison; Trotsky selected it at random to use on a false passport while escaping from his first Siberian exile in 1902. Five years later, having been banished for life to Obdorskoe for his role in the failed revolution of '05, Trotsky escaped again, fleeing six hundred miles across snow-covered tundra in a sleigh pulled by reindeer to reach the Urals, where he posed as a polar explorer to fool the local police.

Stucky's own getaway from Los Angeles would be less

dramatic. By sundown, if all went well, he would be back on his sofa in Seattle with a cup of mint tea and a good book to read, listening to the gentle patter of rain along his roof. He seemed to feel, in the depths of his hangover and the terminal's cavernous silence, that something had been taken from him. But nothing had been taken. He was free to resume his life as it had been before; he could begin trying to write something new. Later—in a few days, when he was settled again—he might call Raskin to demand some answers—though Raskin could indeed be anywhere in the world by now, and answers were, in any case, not among his many specialties. One did not seek Raskin out in order to get answers.

Planes fell, planes rose. The woman on the PA sang her lonely siren song, calling Mr. García, Mr. Wilfredo García, to the nearest white courtesy phone. Her voice sounded exactly like a recording, though of course it could not be. Stucky's head ached—a dull, oceanic pain, throbbing in sluggish time with his pulse. His throat tickled unpleasantly. It was already dry again. The parched cabin air would do him no favors on the trip north. In the foreground of his view, just beneath the window, two idle baggage handlers were miming a heated game of one-on-one. Stucky watched the man in possession of the phantom ball dribble between his legs, fake left, spin right, and toss up a fade-away jumper. His eyes traced the ball's imaginary arc as it soared toward the hoop. He waited; his opponent waited. Stucky waited too. The shooter threw his arms in the air.

Apparently the shot had gone in.

IN THE
ABSENCE OF
PREDATORS

Driving north. I'm driving north, and I feel fine: Connecticut, Massachusetts, New Hampshire. Little towns drift past, charming, colonial places, saltbox architecture. I admire the church steeples and simple buildings—their wholesome austerity, their right angles and straight lines—but I don't stop. The miles fall away. Rolling hills, deep woods, an ocean of trees. Snow begins falling, then falling harder, but I keep moving and I feel fine until the accident.

The accident happens like this: crest a rise on the highway and there she is, no avoiding her. A doe. She begins to move just before the collision, but I catch her in the flank with the right side of my grille, spinning her onto the shoulder. The Buick's back end skids out of control in the opposite direction. I take my hand off the wheel and allow the car to turn 180 degrees, plowing backwards into a highway-side snow bank, headlights pointing back at the prostrate animal. Quiet, wind, snow falling, no other cars. The deer isn't making any hasty moves.

I open the door. Cold stings my cheeks and the silence seems to grow louder as I step out into it. My legs are unsteady as I approach the motionless animal. Neck twisting at a strange angle, limbs bending in unusual places, entrails trailing from the point of impact, snow stained red like Italian ice. The doe is extremely dead. Snowflakes fall into the primary wound and melt there immediately. The eyes, of course, stare wildly into nothing, frozen in anticipation. The strain of terror animates the doe's face in a way no taxidermist or constructor of museum dioramas will ever be able to duplicate. It is, in a word, beautiful, and its beauty seems to bring the night alive.

I stand there looking at the body for a long time.

There's an electric tingle in my extremities and behind my eyes when I return to the car. Like the deer, the Buick has no intention of going anywhere. One of its wheels is caught in a ditch and there's no getting it out. I find, oddly, that this does not disappoint me. I find that I am not upset. To the contrary, as I begin walking down the highway I'm struck by a sense of good fortune, the conviction that I am under the guidance of some benevolent force. The blizzard steps itself up, imposing a new topography of drifts and valleys on the landscape. The snow devours sound. My feet stop crunching and the wind loses its whistle, but I can still feel it on my face and it feels good. Now we're getting somewhere, I think. Now we're on our way.

How far do I walk? Miles, I would say, but it might be less, it might be more, it might be anything. No cars pass in either direction and the diner is the first thing I come to, the first outpost of civilization in the forest. My socks are soaked, my ears are numb. The mucus is frozen inside my nose. Twin Pines Diner, the sign says, Open 24 Hours. The snow is deep now. There are four cars in the lot and they look like Egyptian ruins in the process of being reclaimed by the desert's shifting sands. It takes all the strength I have left to pull the door open through the drift piling against it.

There are four people inside—three men and a boy, an adolescent. One of the men stands behind the counter in a white apron and paper cap, and the others sit on stools, bellied up to the Formica countertop. The place smells of coffee and breakfast meats. It has a certain quality of anachronism, a feeling of obsolescence and nostalgia: mini-jukeboxes in each red leatherette booth, the blood red of the leatherette itself, the accordion-door phone booth in the corner, the checkerboard tile on the floor, the Formica, the paper hat. The rotating vertical pie case reminds me of vacations in the family station wagon when I was young—young enough for the sight of meringue glistening beneath a naked bulb to stir powerful desires.

The three men and the boy are all staring at me with their mouths open, as if I were a tabloid celebrity or an amputee. They form an odd group.

The boy wears a blazer with some sort of crest or coat of arms on the pocket—a heraldic lion or bird of prey. He has red hair, and it's difficult to tell if he's short for his age or just short. He might be the son of the man in the hound's-tooth jacket, but the two do not occupy adjacent stools.

The would-be father is tan despite the geography and season. His build suggests membership in a health club, perhaps the retention of a personal trainer. He sports an olive turtleneck beneath the jacket.

Between him and the boy is a slightly younger man, maybe in his middle thirties, whose face somehow implies the presence of grizzly scars beneath his clothing. Is it the hunch in his shoulders? The narrow cast of his eyes? He wears a navy pea coat and a two-day beard.

The counter man is the oldest of the bunch. He looks to be pushing sixty, with a deeply lined face and large eyes. Like many large-eyed people and veterans of restaurant work, he projects a certain world weariness, a sense of sadness and wisdom. He uses his rag to wipe down a sugar dispenser without looking, as if the action has become automatic.

"Didn't see your car pull in, mister," he says, putting down the sugar and picking up the salt.

"Trouble with the car," I tell him. "Had to walk a ways." The words come out a little sloppy. My lips are numb from the cold.

The old man beckons me to come sit, and I do. He pours

me a cup of coffee. I wrap my hands around the warm mug, moving my face into the path of its steam. Closing my eyes, I can still feel everybody watching me. A nebulous tension fills the room, but I decide that it's only curiosity—the kind that attaches itself to any group of stranded travelers, that special force of boredom responsible for the moral lassitude of airport bars.

I take a couple sips to thaw my mouth out and say, "I hit a deer." I perform a crude reenactment on the countertop; my coffee mug plays the Buick and a thimble of non-dairy creamer is the doe. The creamer topples, rolling awkwardly with its ungainly shape. I pick it up, peel back the lid, and dump the contents into my cup. "My car is stuck in the snow."

There is a general nodding.

"Like every damn car in the state tonight," says the turtleneck guy. He claps me on the back in a way I don't necessarily like. Real chummy, as if we're old yachting pals, or classmates from Andover. "All of us are up shit creek." He laughs, but nobody else does. His chuckle has a nervous pitch. I shoot him a look and the hand drops away. His eyes, I see, are shifty and small, jumping around inside their bronze sockets. "I don't think the tow trucks are running tonight," he adds, looking away, jabbing a thumb into his mouth to chew the nail.

"No," I say, observing the smoky designs of creamer in coffee, "I don't suppose they are."

"The phone is out," says Pea Coat, "even if there were someone for you to call." Does he speak with some kind of foreign accent—something Eastern European, some fiefdom of the Russian mob? Difficult to tell; the hard edge in his voice is faint. It might simply have been caused by a past dental misfortune, like a blow to the mouth from a crowbar. His eyes are bright and not jumping anywhere. "And where were you going on a night like this?" he asks me.

I pause over the question. Going, I think. Going going going. "I'm going to Charlotte," I say, "to be with my family."

"Long trip," Turtleneck points out. He gives a low whistle.

"My family needs me," I say.

"Well, you're lucky then," says the old counter man, "and in the meantime, it's a good thing you found us. You could've died out in that storm."

A brief silence follows, allowing these words to hang in the air. The coffee is thick and acidic, like coffee in a diner should be.

It's the boy who speaks next. His voice is high and nasal. "The human body has the capacity for extraordinary endurance. In 1978 a Norwegian man survived the crash of his prop plane, but was stranded on the beach of some deserted fjord for five nights. This is up around the Arctic Circle. He had no food, no source of warmth. An oyster boat eventually rescued him, but nobody could explain how he'd stayed alive that long. Some considered it a miracle, in the literal sense." The boy pauses to sip his coffee. "That's 'literal' with an 'e', not 'littoral' with an 'o'."

"All the same," says the old man, "I'm glad you made it here. Name's Frank Maxwell. I own this place." Frank Maxwell offers his hand and I shake it over the counter. The hand is cold, cadaverous, strong.

This starts up a round of formal greeting. Pea Coat says to call him Martin, but it's not clear if this is a first name, a last name, or just what I should call him. Turtleneck, meanwhile, introduces himself as Howard C_____, and his surname is immediately familiar to us all, I'm sure, by virtue of the international manufacturing conglomerate that's been operating under it for more than a hundred years. When I ask if he belongs to this corporation's founding (and still controlling) family, Howard responds with a curt nod. "I do," he admits. Anxiety haunts the edge of his voice, as if this might be a burdensome, dangerous fact. The boy, on the other hand, is of no relation — despite his age, he is, like the rest of us, apparently traveling alone. The boy's name is Lewis Fountain and he claims to be fourteen years old.

Another lull in the conversation. Outside, the storm intensifies. Snow presses against the bottoms of the waist-high windows that ring the dining room. The cars have almost disappeared, only their tops protrude. But the eerie quiet persists, lending the blizzard a silent film quality, an element of the unreal.

"My friend," says Martin, perhaps following my eyes, "you will not get out of here anytime soon. Relax, have a drink. Settle in." He produces a pewter flask from inside the pea coat and slides it along the counter.

I pick the flask up and observe the inscription, etched on its front side in a looping script: *To Our Daughter, Good Luck.* Unscrewing the cap, I inhale a pleasantly familiar odor. "Thanks,"

I say. "No place I'd rather be." And it's almost true.

I take a healthy swig and pass the flask to Maxwell, who does the same and passes it on to Howard. Howard swallows his sip and pauses, but then goes ahead and hands the whiskey along to Lewis Fountain, who dumps a shot into his coffee and removes a package of French cigarettes from behind the coat of arms. The polished chrome of his lighter catches the shine of the lamps overhead, flashing like a mirror in the sun.

"Gauloises?" he offers, holding out the pack.

Martin extracts a smoke and sticks it in the corner of his mouth. He leans in to accept a light from the boy and then turns back to me. "I would like to ask you something more," he says, exhaling through his nose. "If you don't mind, I would like to ask what happened to the deer. In your accident, I mean."

For a moment I'm struck by the strange feeling that the question is intensely personal. The mangled deer carcass lies misshapen in the snow of my short-term memory. Martin stares at me with fixed intensity, more expectant than overtly threatening. "She died," I say.

"Yes," he replies, nodding, looking down at his hands. "She died. I suppose she did. It is not a surprise."

"They usually do," Lewis Fountain interjects, tapping his cigarette on the edge of an ashtray. "Ninety percent of all collisions with an automobile are fatal for deer. Read that some-place. Strange animals," he says. "Strange animals."

"Yes," Martin agrees, "and interesting as well. To me, they are quite interesting." He pauses, and something about the way he does so gathers the room's energy around him. When he begins again, his voice is measured, its cadence nice and slow.

I am a drifter. I have no home. When I was eleven I stowed away on a merchant ship to Japan, and this was the last I saw of my parents. Also of my brother and two sisters. I have been without a family since that day.

I have seen death. I have seen more of it than I care to remember, more than a man should. I have seen men shot, hanged, trampled, drowned at sea, consumed by fire. In Turin, I watched a drunk climb into the bear cage at a carnival for a joke.

I have been many places, and I have seen death.

It was very cold where I grew up. Long winters. Father wanted us to be hockey players, and we skated before learning to walk. He took my brother and I out to the lake each afternoon. He dreamed that we would play for the national team, but of course we never did.

One day, when we had finished our practicing, I skated off alone. I was six, maybe seven. Quite young. I skated off alone to a little cove in the lakeshore, an inlet at the mouth of a stream, and there was a buck in the water there. It was huge — ten point, twelve point. Maybe more. I know that memory causes things to grow larger, but its head was the size of my entire body. It was standing in the water almost to its neck, very still. Perfectly still, even as I got close.

I was a fearless, stupid child. I got very close. And then I saw that it was dead. I do not think I even knew what death was until that moment, but suddenly I understood that the buck had died, and I also understood what this meant.

It sounds curious, I know, but the force of this revelation sticks in my head to this day: life is a thing with a beginning and an end.

But it seemed like a miracle to me. The buck was frozen in the ice, hard to the touch. Its fur was frozen, its mouth—to touch them was irresistible. I put my hands all over the animal's body. Icicles hung from the nostrils, the antlers, the lips.

The Lord knows how this could have happened, how it could have died standing up just like that, but nobody can tell me it is impossible.

Nobody can tell me this.

But there is one part—one part that seems as if I must have dreamed it, although I swear that I did not. Who knows what tricks the memory will play. Still, what I recall more vividly than anything is the blood, which was suspended in a cloud just beneath the surface of the ice, like frozen red smoke.

Can you imagine this?

A suspended explosion, right beneath my feet, trapped in the ice. I remember kneeling down, pressing my face close to look. The color of it. It was the first I saw of death, and caused me to think, from that very young age, that death is beautiful.

Martin finishes and stabs his smoke out in the ashtray, a movement of controlled violence. He smiles—sadly, I think, the way a man smiles when he looks back on a life filled with terrible mistakes. Shaking his head, he puts the flask back to work, swallows, puts it to work again.

What does this story mean? It seems like a gesture of sudden, bizarre intimacy, and each of us is left to separately consider the altered dynamic of our marooned group. I stare into my mug and the dregs of my coffee stare back. Maxwell tugs his rag along the counter, bobbing his head faintly to some internal thought or rhythm. The coffeemaker goes: drip-drop, drip-drop.

Then Lewis Fountain says, "But it's not." We all turn to him. "Beautiful, I mean. A lot of things are beautiful, but death isn't one of them." He looks away. "Or at least I sure as hell don't think it is," he adds, fumbling now for the Gauloises, flashing a shy smile.

I watch Martin eyeing the boy through those narrowed lids. He runs the backside of his fingers up one cheek, against the grain of his beard. "Go on," he says.

Lewis Fountain lights his cigarette with a sheltering hand cupped around the flame, as if there were a breeze in the breeze-less room. He closes the Zippo with a deliberate motion and squints at us through blue haze. "Look at me," he says. We look. Red hair, freckles. A face we've all seen in our school yearbooks, staring out from group photos of the debate team, the Quiz Bowl squad, the chess club.

I'm fourteen years old. What do I know about death? All four of my grandparents are still alive. But there was an incident at my school not long ago. St. Delamore Hall. You probably know the name.

Our campus backs up on the woods. When I say that deer are strange animals, I speak from experience. They come around all the time. Hunting's not in style anymore, and most of their natural predators were driven out a long time ago. So there's too many of them. Rats with antlers—that's what the townies say. They chew up gardens, get into trash.

And they spook easy. Anything can set them off: a siren, a dog whistle, sunlight on a windshield. We were in the dining hall at lunch one day, and there was a deer out on the rugby field. It was acting strange, running back and forth— hyperkinetic, unnatural. There was something real unnatural about the way that thing moved.

The dining hall has a bank of windows at the south end, and we were all watching this deer. You couldn't look away—like a car wreck, I guess, although I've never seen a car wreck except on TV. A doe. Its head was twitching, its ears, its nose. Real crazy. Back and forth, back and forth, and then it turned and stared in the window. It stopped running around and looked directly into the dining hall. Almost like it had realized we were watching. Like it could feel us watching.

And then it started running toward us.

You should have been there. At first people were laughing, but then the whole room got quiet. Real quiet. And then it came through the window. It jumped straight through the window and landed in front of the salad bar.

Wonder the deer didn't die right there either, but it

didn't. Lots of blood, but it got up and ran out into the hallway. You could hear it going berserk out there. Created a hell of a stir, and none of the teachers knew what to do. They just closed the doors and told us to stay put.

I got out through the service entrance.

You want to talk about beauty? I'll tell you what that hallway looked like. It looked like it was bleeding. The floor, the walls, the lockers. They were all bleeding.

That doe must have run through four times in each direction, looking for a way out. There was so much blood that it was hard for me to follow the trail. She had gone in and out of the chem lab and Dr. Kroft's Latin classroom, made circles in the front lobby. The panic must have been insane.

Totally insane.

I found her in the girls' locker room, collapsed in the shower. She was cut to ribbons, not dead but getting there. Too weak to move, shivering from the blood loss. There was so much blood the drain gurgled with it.

It was one of those big gang showers, twenty nozzles on the wall and three drains in the middle of the floor. She was lying in the corner, so I sat down next to her and waited. Everybody else was still locked in the dining hall and the Animal Control people weren't there yet.

Gurgle, gugle—that was it. That and the doe trying to breather.

I don't know how long I was in there. Ten minutes, an hour. The guys from the county showed up eventually with their tranquilizer guns, but there wasn't anything left for them to do. I spent the rest of the day with the school psychologist, talking *about how I want to fuck my mother or whatever. Goddamn two-bit quack.*

Smoke rings. Lewis Fountain blows four of them, then shoots a miniature fifth ring through the last one's empty center.

Martin holds out the flask. "When did all this happen?" he asks.

The boy takes a slug. "Yesterday," he says. "I stole one of the school vans this afternoon and started driving."

Interesting. Maxwell takes the coffee pot off its burner and pours us all another round. "That storm doesn't look like it means to let up," he says. "I don't suppose the cops'll find you. Not tonight, anyway." He smiles at the boy. His smile is thin, touched by a certain complexity.

"They'll never take me," says Lewis Fountain.

Installing a fresh smoke in the corner of his mouth, he wrist-flicks the lighter open and rolls it smartly on his thigh to spark the flame. Leaning back, he empties the remainder of the whiskey into his coffee.

"Jesus," Howard says, standing up, "we need more liquor." He gestures to Lewis Fountain, tapping two fingers against his mouth. "Gimme one of those." The boy holds out the Gauloises, shaking the pack until a single filter protrudes. Howard snaps it up, stabs it into his mouth, snatches the lighter, and clicks three times before the flint catches. He puffs twice, sneering slightly, but you can tell by the way he smokes that Howard is no smoker. He holds the butt a little too stiffly in his hand, and places it too much in the center of his mouth.

He is sweating. Droplets collect in his eyebrows and bead on his nose. "I've got a story too," he says. "I've got a story of my own." He begins pacing the aisle in front of the counter. We have to turn all the way around on our stools to face him. We wait. His penny loafers slap the tile, slap the tile, slap the tile.

Last year. This was last year, in Vermont. I was driving back from Stowe and it was late and snowing. A night kind of like this. Not a blizzard, I guess, but it was snowing alright, snowing plenty.

I was on a little two-lane highway outside Irasville, totally deserted. I hit a deer—just like you, friend, I hit a deer. Only the car was fine. The SUV, I should say, and I didn't even hit the damn thing square, but I stopped to see if it was dead or alive. It seemed like the right thing to do.

Seemed like the right thing.

Look, you can all guess the kind of money I grew up with, but that doesn't make me a bad person. Morality has nothing to do with class. My family is well known, powerful, and subject to a great deal of scrutiny. This brings with it a certain set of pressures and challenges, but I'm not asking for sympathy. I've always done my best to fly right and be my own man.

So I stopped to see about the deer, and in fact it was still alive. Still alive, but I had crushed its back legs. They were trailing after the damn thing like a couple of neckties. Totally limp. It had dragged itself off the road using only the front two, and was trying to get back to the woods that way, but it was no go.

*Disturbing as hell to watch. It didn't look real. The way
those animals move—it never looks real to me: jerky, quick,
and then they glide. I don't know. They look like fucking string
puppets or something, and this hurt buck even more so. It was
scary, but I couldn't leave the damn thing that way.*

Didn't seem right.

*There weren't a lot of other cars out there at that
hour—not that there ever are—but I flagged down the first one
that came by and told the guy to call the cops when he got to
town.*

*Then I sat down to wait. I mean I went right out and
sat down in the snow beside that buck. I don't know why, but
that's what I did. He had stopped trying to move. It was cold,
but I had my ski jacket, and I decided just to wait until the
police showed up. Like it was the least I could do or something.
But those cops took their sweet time—an hour passed, two
hours. And the buck wasn't dying either. It just couldn't move.*

*I didn't know what to do, so I started talking to it.
I started telling it things. I just said whatever came into my
head—about my life, about how I was sorry for hitting it, about
whatever. I know it sounds strange, but I had to pass the time
some way. People will do weird things in a spot like that.*

*So I'm talking to this deer. I'm talking and talking. And
then it starts talking back. The damn deer starts talking back
to me. I mean it wasn't actually talking, but it was blinking
its eyes—like Morse code or something.*

*And what's more, I started to understand what it was
saying. Not directly, but I started to get this idea in my head of*

what the deer was trying to tell me. I can't explain it—you're all gonna think I'm nuts, but there was this idea in my head, and I hadn't put it there myself. I'm telling you, that deer was talking to me. It was inside my fucking head.

The damn thing was telling me to kill it.

I tried. There was a crowbar in the back of my Navigator, so I went and got it. I went and got it and stood there over that goddamn buck.

Hell of a thing to kill.

Hell of a thing to kill.

I took a swing—a good swing. Hit it dead in the face. But that didn't do the trick. Set the thing twitching and freaking out, but didn't kill it. Snapped its jaw—the bone was hanging out with a few teeth flapping in the wind.

But I couldn't finish it. The way that blow felt going up my arms, the sound of its bones cracking. I just sat back down in the snow and watched that fucking deer twitching and flopping with its jawbone hanging out.

Cops got there after a while. They just walked right up and shot it like taking out the garbage. No ceremony whatsoever. Told jokes while they did it. Like taking out the fucking garbage.

Is Howard crying? He hands his butt to Lewis Fountain, apparently for disposal, and bites his finger like a child. Nobody says anything. It's hard to distinguish tears from sweat, but the quiet jerking of his shoulders touches the place in my memory occupied by a thousand moments of domestic strife. We all look away.

Maxwell is wiping down the napkin dispenser. We wait. He stops wiping and examines his reflection in the polished chrome. Howard blows his nose. Lewis Fountain lights another cigarette. Martin is rubbing his hands together slowly, back and forth, back and forth. The old man sighs and takes off his paper hat. His forehead is large, giving way eventually to sparse gray hair. "Shit," he says, drawing a bottle out from underneath the counter. Scotch—and not the kind they drink in Bridgehampton. We pass it around, and the stuff goes down easy as a clump of steel wool. Maxwell drinks last and longest. He does it like a man who knows his way around a bottle of bad Scotch.

"Sometimes it feels like I've been alive forever," he says, "forever and a goddamn day." His eyes stare out over our heads, as if all that time might be visible in the distance, a circus parade silhouetted against the horizon. "But I was only in love once. Maybe one time is all anybody really gets. I don't know. I was young and full of shit, and I was in love."

"And was she beautiful?" Martin asks.

"Sure," Maxwell says, "sure, why not. Very beautiful."

"What did she look like?" Howard wants to know. He dabs at his cheeks with a linen handkerchief.

"Close your eyes," Maxwell tells him, and we all close our eyes. "Now picture the first girl you were ever in love with," the old man says. But that's not what I do. I do not picture Veronica Phipps glossing her lips in the back row of trigonometry class, lovely and pliable as she was in the matinee balconies and cow pastures of forever ago. I picture my wife instead: Helen building castles with our children on a sun-drenched strip of Carolina Beach; Helen in the window of a French restaurant, laughing at the joke of some greasy waiter, flashing her open-ended smile; Helen with that coffee mug raised above her head, cocked to throw; Helen in the glare of my headlights in the snow; Helen behind the wheel of a late-model Buick, cresting a rise on the highway, bearing down on me at a high rate of speed. "Looked about like that," Maxwell says, "only he wasn't a girl. He definitely wasn't a girl."

The old man pauses for two beats and a shadow moves across him, a faint darkening of the features, those big eyes wandering off into the snowstorm night.

This was a long time ago, a long way from here. Northeast Ohio, what they now call the Rust Belt, and you better believe they call it that for a reason. We were just finding out back then. Hard times. Hard to explain too, the way it felt.

Our mill had just closed down. Wasn't much left after that. A lot of people were leaving, but the ones who stayed were leaving too. Every week another car would drive into the river. Or an old woman would freeze to death, couldn't pay the utility. Or somebody else would hang himself in a barn.

Some just disappeared.

I guess hard times are like that anywhere. Same thing happened sooner or later to all those factory towns — happened to Pittsburgh, even — but it was strange enough to watch. Everybody looked older than they should have, like the whole damn place was turning into a ghost of itself.

My father sold shoes, but people stopped buying shoes. He hit the bottle and it hit him back. This boy, this boy I had, his father shut himself in the basement day after the mill closed, and didn't come out. He'd been a shift foreman, doing pretty well for himself. Had a big Brunswick pool table down in that cellar, and what I remember best about their house is the sound of the balls clicking against each other underneath you.

It was always there, soft, so you might not even notice it exactly. But it was always there, even late. Any time of the night.

His wife had to bring the money in, so she started a little business hand-making these special dolls. Fancy ones, real life-like. Sold them to high-end toy stores in Cleveland. God knows where she ever learned to do a thing like that. I can see her like yesterday, sitting at the dining room table with a pile of horse manes from the knacker's yard. That's how she did the hair. Damn house was disturbing as hell, and I never liked to go there.

You can imagine what it was to be in love in a place like that, especially the way we had to hide it. Nowadays you can't turn on the television without seeing faggots on parade. They're everywhere. Things were different then.

Had a place in the woods where we'd go to be alone, a hunting cabin I knew. Just a lean-to, a falling down shack. No heat, no way to make a fire. This was winter and we would hike in from the road with a sleeping bag. I'm sure there was someplace easier we could have gone. Always snow on the ground in those days, and the walk was at least a mile. But that cabin was our spot and we went there. Couldn't say exactly

why. I guess it was partly the silence of the woods in winter.
Nothing else like it in the world.

But that wasn't the strange part. Biggest window in the
cabin was on the western wall where the sun came in afternoons.
It went right down to the floor, and that was where we always
spread the bag out. And that's how I started noticing the deer.
Or how the deer started noticing us.

Through the window.

Sometimes it was just one or two, sometimes more. Once
I counted six. At first I would only hear them moving away
when we had finished, but then I started looking. As soon as we
began, they'd be there, standing and watching.

Just standing and watching.

The four of us are sitting and watching, bodies perched on the
edges of our stools. We wait to see if Maxwell will say more, but
he falls quiet.

"Were you afraid?" Howard asks, looking afraid himself.

The old man shakes his head, a slow and definite motion.
"Not of the deer. Maybe at first, but after a while it seemed to
make sense."

"But it doesn't," Howard protests. "It doesn't make any
damn sense."

Maxwell opens his hands and spreads them apart, palms
up. "It seemed to at the time."

"And this boy?" Martin inquires. "What became of this
boy?"

Maxwell's eyes return to the room. They make a full

circuit of it, not in any kind of rush. "We got found out."

He begins to fold his hat on the Formica, first one way, then the other. That noise of paper rustling, like wind kicking up dead leaves. "I guess it was inevitable. Some things happened that weren't very pleasant."

"And you left," I say. It's the first I've spoken in a long time. The sound of my voice is sudden and strange, spilled out in a jumble on the countertop.

"Yes," Maxwell answers. His lips curl briefly into a smile, but not the happy kind. "And I never went back."

Never, I think, turning the word over in my brain, examining it from various angles. Never never never never never.

"What was his name?" Lewis Fountain asks, speaking through his lovely blue cloud.

"Theodore," Maxwell says, not very loud. "His name was Theodore." The sound of these words drifts away — I feel that I can see it drifting, dissipating into the night like coffee steam, cigarette smoke. Like anything that floats off and dissolves.

Silence descends on us again, like a bird of prey, silence like death itself. I become aware, as the quiet intensifies, that my feet are itching and my head hurts. My mouth is a little dry. That liquor hasn't done me any favors, and neither has the burly coffee. I can't remember the last time I ate or had a shower. But none of this alarms me; it all seems to just be part of the situation, like the weather, the checkered floor tiles, the stale smell of smoke, the way Martin sits with one palm pressed against his temple and his dark eyes closed. Looking down, I see that my own clothes are disheveled. My shirt is half untucked, my shoes both untied. My pricey wristwatch is no longer on my wrist. Looking up, I see Maxwell staring hard into the middle distance again.

I begin to wonder how I got here.

Fear gets inside of you, I know, and eats away the best part of what you have. Sitting there on my stool in the Twin Pines Diner, I'm struck by a force of nostalgia so powerful that it causes my body to shudder, and this too, I think, is a kind of fear, an apprehension that the best of life is behind you.

You see it all the time. Does anybody remember, says the old woman on the bus, when they gave me a tiara and made me queen of the strawberry festival? Nobody does. The other passengers turn away, pretending not to hear. She must be crazy, senile, ineffectively medicated. But her emotions are not unfamiliar—all she really means is that her happiness ended too soon, like happiness always does, and she wants to hold onto the memories. So why not offer a little sympathy?

But then again, why are you all alone on this bus, Strawberry Queen, babbling to yourself in a foul-smelling housecoat? Where's your family, with all your blue-eyed grandchildren, who wrestle each other for the right to sit on your knee? What have you done to drive them away?

My own memories are simple, or at least they travel in simple images—Helen in the shadows of our porch, the children playing in our yard. That kind of thing. I think back to summertime vacations down at the shore, all of us piling into the station wagon and arriving by evening at the carnival there on the promenade, which seemed at the time like an extension of our hopefulness, our faith in life: the smell of cotton candy, the arc of the Ferris wheel, the spinning teacups on the teacup ride. Gaudy colors, giddy music, the laughter of euphoric kids. Standing on the boardwalk at night, the lights were like a magician's trick, throwing strange shapes on the ocean, designs that would shimmer and shift. Concentrating on the seductive power of these recollections, I can almost feel the light breeze that would come up off the water, stirring an ancient sense of possibility in the soul, something from the depths of our cultural subconscious, from somewhere far back in the seafaring history of man.

But maybe it wasn't that way at all.

Maybe my son threw up on the tilt-o-whirl, and a clown scared my daughter half to death with his balloon animals, the suggestiveness and obscenity of their shapes, and we eventually found ourselves standing there, Helen and I, drenched in the rancid water of the log flume, arguing over which one of us had locked the keys in the car while the children wailed like air-raid sirens at our feet.

Or maybe we never really went to the shore at all, and I'm just thinking of some movie I've seen, something Disney about a square-jawed hero and his obedient, adoring family, or else maybe a slasher flick in which the clowns all carry butcher knives in their oversized red shoes.

"I lied," says Howard, very quiet now. "I lied before about what that deer was telling me. It wasn't telling me to kill it."

He tilts his head back, fixes his eyes on the ceiling. "It was telling me to kill myself."

The words settle in the room like snow.

I don't know who sees them first. It seems, although I know this is unlikely, as if we all see them at exactly the same moment, emerging from the darkness outside the diner's lights, a disparate movement in the nighttime at first, coalescing into a throng of shadows advancing in unison, as if possessed of a single consciousness. There are hundreds of them: bucks, does, little knock-kneed fawns. There may be thousands, coming forward, their outlines gradually gaining faces, their dark eyes becoming visible, but still in perfect silence.

"Teddy," Maxwell whispers. "Teddy, Teddy, Teddy."

There is only that, and then finally the sound of the velvet of their antlers tapping on the glass of the windows slowly, slowly, gentle at first.

ACKNOWLEDGMENTS

Thank you to the following publications where these stories—
or earlier versions—first appeared:

Esquire online: "White Dog"

Mississippi Review online: "The Crying of the Gulls"

The Virginia Quarterly Review: "Fauntleroy's Ghost"

Harvard Review: "In the Absence of Predators"

**RESCUE
+PRESS**